Step by Wicked Step

Books by Anne Fine

Alias Madame Doubtfire

My War with Goggle-eyes

The Book of the Banshee

The Chicken Gave It to Me

Flour Babies

Step by Wicked Step

Step by Wicked Step

A Novel by ANNE FINE

Little, Brown and Company
Boston   New York   Toronto   London

First U.S. Edition

Library of Congress Cataloging-in-Publication Data

Fine, Anne.
    Step by Wicked Step : a novel / by Anne Fine. — 1st U.S. ed.
       p.   cm.
    Summary: Five schoolmates share the stories of their parents'
estrangements, divorces, and remarriages and the effects these
events have had on their lives.
    ISBN 0-316-28345-2
    [1. Divorce — Fiction. 2. Stepfamilies — Fiction. 3. Remarriage —
Fiction.]   I. Title.
    PZ7.F459673St   1996
    [Fic] — dc20   95-43251

10 9 8 7 6 5 4 3 2 1

MV-NY

Printed in the United States of America

Step by
Wicked Step

$\mathcal{E}$ven before they reached the haunted house, the night had turned wild. The face of the minivan driver flickered from blue to white under the lightning. Each peal of thunder made the map in Mr. Plumley's hand shiver. And the five leftover pupils from Stagfire School peered anxiously through the rain-spattered windows into the storm and the black night.

"There!"

"Where?"

"Over there. See? Up that overgrown driveway."

As the driver swung the minivan into the looming hole between the wrought-iron gates, the three on the right-hand side of the bus made out the words on the peeling sign.

"Old Harwick Hall."

"Absolutely private."

"No trespassers. No circulars."

Colin, who had been quiet the whole journey, suddenly spoke.

"That's friendly! They don't even want you coming up their drive to give them a free paper!"

Everyone stared out, flinching as the twisted fingers of trees scraped at the glass. After the terrible journey, somebody might have said, "I'm glad we're here," but no one was sure they were. If they'd been lucky enough to travel on the bus with everyone else, they might have felt more of a crowd; they might have had fewer misgivings. But just the five of them, picked out by Miss O'Dell after a quick glance at her list, and herded in the minivan with Mr. Plumley like leftovers shoved in the fridge — well, that was different.

Another brilliant flash lit up a jagged stone tower, strangled by ivy.

"Is that it?"

"No, that's the old chapel."

They'd all heard about the ruined chapel. It was forbidden ground, and if you were caught climbing on its perilously steep slopes, you were sent home, even though this was a school week. All they could see of it from the minivan as they swept by was a dark silhouette of tumbled stone.

"Yikes!" the driver said suddenly, stabbing at the brakes.

Everyone turned from the side windows and stared ahead.

"There it is!"

"Oh, my!"

Through the arcs of the wipers, they could make out a towering mansion with dunce-hatted turrets, standing black against storm clouds. Moonlight flickered eerily against its dark windows.

"Creepsville!"

"Maybe it really *is* haunted . . ."

(No one had truly believed it, up till now. It was just something the last group always came back with: tales of strange shadows and footsteps, and eerie figures in white gowns melting through walls. Each year, at least three people in every class swore — spit and hope to die! — that they had seen a ghost.)

The driver swung around in her seat.

"Well," she asked Mr. Plumley, "are you getting them all out?"

Not giving him time to answer, she took charge herself, sliding open the side door. Everyone spilled out. They took the luggage from the back of the van ("Don't stop to look for your own bag!" the driver ordered. "Just take the nearest!") and splashed through the puddles to the shelter of the steep-roofed porch. Here, out of the driving rain, they exchanged battered duffel bags and brand-new backpacks as the driver took off in a spray of wet gravel, and their teacher stared miserably at the huge oak-and-iron door.

"Ring the bell, Mr. Plumley," prompted Claudia.

"What bell?"

Quite right. No bell that anyone could see.

"Try knocking, then."

Rob knocked the hardest. But it was clear to everyone that, if they could barely hear his fierce hammering over the whine of the wind, no one inside would even notice it.

"Try the handle," suggested Pixie.

Obediently, Mr. Plumley twisted the heavy ring handle, and pushed. The door grated open, over a black-and-white tiled floor that looked like a huge checkerboard glazed with storm water.

"Try the lights."

None of the switches did anything. Ralph and Pixie took turns at flicking them up and down. But no lights came on anywhere.

"Storm damage, I guess," said Ralph.

Mr. Plumley was horrified.

"You don't suppose that they'll be off all *night?* It's not going to be easy settling you all in one of the dormitories in the pitch dark."

The thunder crashed so loudly that nobody cared to mention they'd all made plans to sleep in different rooms.

"We'll go up these stairs here — *ouch!*"

Poor Mr. Plumley had marched straight into a giant floor-to-ceiling mirror that reflected the wide curve of stairs sweeping out of the shadows behind them.

He turned to face the other direction.

"This way," he said.

The five of them trailed up the vast staircase after Mr. Plumley. Each livid flash of lightning through the stained glass above their heads lit their way further up, and further on, through the huge, echoing mansion. Fronds of strange plants stretched from their pots and fingered them as they passed. Disturbed ornaments chattered on mahogany sideboards. And grim Harwicks of all ages stared down at them through hardened, oil-painted eyes.

"Let's try up here."

It was yet another staircase, narrow and bare. They'd left the portraits and the carpets behind them now. Their footsteps clattered on the wooden steps as they spiraled up and up.

"Ah! This will do."

He had pushed open a door, and found a little tower room with beds pointing neatly toward the center from five of the six walls.

"But, Mr. Plumley —"

Pixie nudged Claudia, hard. Claudia might want the two of them to go off on their own, up some other lonely dark tower, rather than break one of the strictest of the rules: *Each bedroom is for either girls or boys.* But on a night like this, with Miss O'Dell and the others still not here, Pixie preferred safety in numbers.

Mr. Plumley turned back.

"What is it, Claudia?"

Claudia's heart stopped, as sheets of rain lashed at the window panes, and the wind howled.

"Nothing, Mr. Plumley."

It wasn't their fault if he hadn't bothered to learn the rules for the week the class went on their field trip.

"You settle down. I'll go and see if I can find what the housekeeper has left us for supper."

A peal of thunder stopped him at the door.

"Anyone want to come with me?" he asked them hopefully.

"No, thank you, Mr. Plumley," everyone said.

He set off bravely down the narrow stairs.

Pixie sat on a bed.

"Horrible!" she said. "Horrible! Horrible! Horrible!"

Nobody knew if she meant the bed, the house, the storm, or all three. Nobody asked. Rob propped the door open with his bag, and went on a prowl, up two or three more stairs and around another bend. His voice echoed cheerfully through the next roll of thunder.

"There are two more beds up here, and a bathroom. The tub's enormous. It has feet with claws."

"I know what I need," said Claudia. "Is there a —?"

"Yes!" More lightning flashed. "And it has a gold chain with a china handle that says 'PULL.'"

Claudia was out of the door in a moment. Pixie ran after her. And Colin went up, too. Ralph made sure that Rob's duffel bag stayed in the doorway, propping it open till they were all safely back again.

Then they sat in the dark with their legs dangling over the ends of the beds: a tight little circle, like campers around a dead fire.

"Should we unpack?" asked Rob. "We three could stay here, and Claudia and Pixie could have those two beds up the stairs."

"What's the point?" Ralph asked. "We all have plans to share with other people. We'll only have to pack up and move when Miss O'Dell and the others come."

"*If* they come . . ."

"What's the time?"

Ralph held the face of his watch toward a window, waiting for lightning.

"Nine forty-five," he told them, at the next flash.

"Lights out by ten-thirty," Claudia reminded them.

"That's all right," Pixie said bitterly. "They probably still will be." She hugged herself as another brilliant flare of light ripped open the sky, and flooded the tower room with incandescent silver.

They all looked paler in the dark that followed. But Colin was pointing at the wall, just behind Claudia's head.

"Look!"

Everyone turned.

"What?"

"I can't see anything."

"What's the matter?"

"Look!" Colin said again. "In the wall. It's a door. There's a door hidden in the wall."

"Where?"

"There's nothing there, Colin."

"Oh, yes, there is. I saw it."

He crawled over Claudia's bed. In the dark, they could barely make out the shadow of his hands running up and down over the broad stripes of ancient wallpaper.

"I can't see anything."

"Wait," Colin told them. "Sit and wait. You'll see what I saw."

They sat without speaking. Around the tower, the wind still howled, but not so dolefully as before. The storm was moving over.

Five seconds. Ten. And then another flash shot generously across the sky.

And they all saw. The vivid sliver of light picked out the lines where, cleverly, but not quite cleverly enough, the wallpapered door met the wallpapered wall.

Rob rushed over to give it a push. Nothing. Claudia ran her fingers over the place, halfway up the wall, where any hidden handle should have been. Nothing again. And Colin said:

"Sit back. And watch again."

Since he'd been right before, everyone obeyed him. They stared through one weakening flash after another, till, just in time, Rob had the sense to step across and tug Claudia's bed a little further from the wall. As the last, far-away burst of light speared through the freshly rinsed panes, each of them finally saw, just where the frame of her bed had hidden it, the strange little telltale pockmark on the wall.

"Go on. Try it."

The peal of thunder chased its bolt of lightning across the sky as Rob leaned forward and pressed.

The door sprang open.

Everybody stared.

It was the tangled veil of stretched and broken cobwebs they noticed first.

"Nobody's been through this door for years and *years*."

"Who's coming in?"

"Not me!"

"Nor me!"

But, as if Rob had cast the spell of his own courage on them, they all crept after him into the tiny room. A tower off a tower. Through the six delicate vaulted windows, as narrow as the ones that archers used, the storm-washed moonlight poured in pale blue shafts. The dust lay thick — on shelf and desk and chair, on lantern and candelabra, on books and cushions — even on the floor, where the brash patterns pressed by the soles of their shoes made them feel even more like trespassers. It was quite obvious to every one of them that no one had stepped into this room as long as anyone alive could possibly remember.

Claudia stretched out a finger toward one of the window ledges, where a tiny carved wooden cow balanced forlornly on three legs. Just as she stroked its nose, trying to comfort it for all those years and years of loneliness, she heard a soft whirring behind her.

"What's that?"

Rob had set a huge varnished globe of the world spinning on its axis.

"Rob! Don't!"

He put out a hand to stop it. Claudia was right. Like a museum or a church, this was no place for idle fun and games.

Ralph gazed at the cobwebs glinting in the moonlight.

"Whose room *was* this, I wonder . . ."

The heavy drapes, the plain dark coverlet, the framed old maps — surely even his frail and nodding great-grandmother had spent her childhood in a brighter room than this. All he could tell from looking around was that, when it was left to spiders all those years ago, the last child to sleep in that high, ornate bed came from a family with a mint of money.

Claudia was peering at the spindly desk.

"This was a boy's room."

"How can you tell?"

Claudia pointed to a dusty green album. As they watched, she leaned forward and, just as if the dull-looking binder on the desk was a delicious birthday cake, studded with candles, she took the most enormous breath, and blew.

Dust flew in clouds. And suddenly all of them could see what, up till then, only Claudia had noticed in spidery writing on the cover.

Richard Clayton Harwick — My Story.
Read and weep.

"Yikes!" Rob said, echoing the driver without thinking. But this reminder of the minivan raised in Ralph's mind an explanation other than dying wind for the faint rumble outside.

"Is that the bus?"

Pixie rushed to the window ledge, and peered down.

"It's in the courtyard. They're getting their stuff out."

Ralph snatched up the album.

"Quick!" he said. "Pixie and Claudia — upstairs! Try and look fast asleep. Rob and Colin — into bed, quickly!"

Rob stared.

"Why?" he demanded. "If Miss O'Dell thinks we're asleep, she'll leave us here, and I won't get to share with my friends."

Pixie turned in the doorway.

"He's right. It was bad enough being taken off the bus. But this way I won't even get a bed next to Shreela."

Ralph pointed around the little tower room, drowned in moonlight and lost time.

"Listen," he begged. "If we come back to read this tomorrow, everyone else will find out. And Miss O'Dell will take charge of the album, and lock the tower room." He spread his hands. "You *know* that," he told them.

They knew that. Nobody argued.

"But we could just pretend to be asleep, and read it tonight. Our friends won't be upset. They'll just think Mr. Plumley told us to stick together in the storm. And by tomorrow we'll be back with them."

Rob still looked unconvinced.

"But *why?*"

"*Why?*" Ralph held the album out toward him with both hands. "Rob, how often do you get a chance like this?"

He ran his fingers over the spidery writing.

"*Richard Clayton Harwick. Read and weep,*" he said softly. "How many people are brave enough to tell you their story?" He was practically begging now. Rob, how many chances do you get to peer into someone else's *life?*"

Rob said nothing, but, backing out through the door, he swept his duffel bag onto the nearest bed, and started to root for his pajamas. The girls fled upstairs, and Colin and Ralph pulled the hidden door closed behind them. By the time Miss O'Dell and Mr. Plumley climbed wearily up the stairs a few minutes later, carrying sandwiches and drinks, all that they saw in the first tower room were three dark mounds under the coverlets.

"Imagine!" said Mr. Plumley. "I'd no idea they were as tired as that."

Miss O'Dell dumped the soda cans on the floor.

"Where are the girls?"

She tiptoed further up the stairs.

"Ah! Here they are. Fast asleep as well."

"Shouldn't we wake them?"

The way Miss O'Dell stared at him, you'd think he'd asked, 'Shouldn't we stab them?'

"Haven't we had enough problems? There might be a bit of a fuss tomorrow, if they can't find beds next to their best friends. But after that frightful journey, I'm not waking *anyone.*"

Pulling the pile of wrapped sandwiches out of Mr. Plumley's arms, she tipped them onto the end of the nearest bed.

"Anyway," she added cheerfully, "these five must have something in common. That's why I picked them out. It didn't seem fair that the only ones not to travel on the bus should be the few who hadn't yet barged rudely onto the last seats. So I just looked at my list, and picked out the first five names with an asterisk in one of the columns."

"Which column?"

Mr. Plumley was interested. It didn't seem to him that little firebrand Pixie had anything in common at all with steady, sensible Claudia. Or that quickwitted and hardworking Ralph was in any way similar to Colin, whose habit of drifting through the hours of each school day as if his thoughts were hundreds of miles away drove all his teachers to despair.

And as for soccer-mad Rob! What this sports-crazy boy might share with any of the rest, Mr. Plumley couldn't imagine.

"Which column?" he asked again.

But Miss O'Dell was already halfway down the stairs. Impatiently, her answer echoed up, prompting him to scuttle down after her.

"How should I know? Maybe they're all vegetarians. Or allergic to wasp stings. Or non-swimmers. I didn't bother to look. But, believe me, even if they don't know it yet, these five have something in common."

And just as the lights came on again all over the house, she shut the tower door, leaving in breath-holding silence five ill-assorted eavesdroppers who, like Mr. Plumley, found that rather hard to believe.

$\mathcal{A}$s soon as Pixie and Claudia had crept back into the room, Ralph slid the album out from under his pillow.

"Who's going to read it?"

Before Claudia could suggest something fair, like tossing a coin, or taking turns, Pixie had stretched out her hands.

"Give it to me. I'm terrific at reading."

Ralph rolled his eyes at her as she snatched the album.

"It can't be modesty we have in common," he teased.

Everyone laughed except Pixie. Pixie just glowered.

"Or finding the same things funny," added Ralph.

Pixie ignored him. She was already opening the book.

"Ssh!" she said, settling herself on the nearest spare bed. "Are you listening?"

And since she was terrific at reading, they soon were.

Richard Clayton Harwick – My Story.
Read and weep.

When I was young, my father took a fever. Day by day, everything changed. A dreadful silence fell upon our house. The maids wept in corners. My mother's dark dresses billowed as she hurried across landings, impatiently snatching from the servants' hands the things she begged my father to lift his head from the pillows and try: poor things indeed! a sip of water, a slice of peach, the tiniest fragment of dry toast. But it was of no use. Nobody said a word to me — what should they say? Everyone loved him so, they would have fallen into fits of weeping saying it! — but early one evening I came across George the gardener leaning heavily on his spade, and took the courage to ask him.

"Mr. Digby. Is my father dying?"

He lifted his head and stared.

"Oh, Master Richard!" he said, pushing the spade aside and crushing me to his breast.

And then I knew.

That night, Lucy the maid came in my mother's place to hear my prayers and say "Good night, God bless." The frills round her apron were damp, and even as she sat at my bedside, her thoughts were far from this little tower room, and she kept dabbing at her eyes.

"Lucy," I asked her, "will it be tonight?"

At once she laid a finger on my lips.

"Hush! Don't even speak of it."

Before I could ask her more, she had jumped to her feet, and hurried away, weeping.

But early next morning, when I had chased the dogs up and down the avenue of lime trees till I, at least, was tired, then hidden myself deep in the shrubbery to be alone with my dark fears, I heard a frantic rustling in the undergrowth, and saw a puff-ball of white frills pushing its way between bushes, and slapping its dainty hands crossly at all the cold dewdrops flying from the leaves. And there in front of me stood little Charlotte.

"Dickie! Mama has set the whole house a-searching. Papa has hugged and kissed me, and now he is asking to see you."

I know my duty to my sister. But I confess I left her rescue to the mercy of the under-gardeners. Without a word of thanks to her for her message, so hard-delivered, I crashed my way out of the shrubbery, sped across the lawns, and took a shortcut through the open french windows.

As I leaped over the rugs, a heavy, black-sleeved hand fell on my arm, swinging me round.

"Stay, boy!"

It was the Reverend Cragley. It was not Sunday, but still I wished him back in his dark, ivy-smothered chapel.

"Sir, I am in a hurry."

He gripped my arm tighter, and loomed over me. His pale face peered into mine. He was dressed black as a bat, and (I'll say it fearlessly, now he has done his best to beat fear out of me) he was no more welcome than one of those sinister, misbegotten creatures would be in my mother's pretty morning room.

"Please, sir! I beg you. My father wishes to see me. I must go."

He pinched my elbow.

"Are these your best manners?"

"Yes, sir," I said sharply. "When I know that my mother has sent for me."

Then he stepped back. There was a flash of anger in those ice-blue eyes. And, when he spoke, his voice was even sharper than mine, with, I sensed, far more practice.

"Trust me," he warned. "I shall take time to mend your manners soon."

On any other day, I might have taken time to disbelieve him. But I just ran — up the stairs and over the landing, to where my mother watched for me in the doorway.

"Richard," she said to me sternly, brushing the unruly hair back from my forehead, "now you must be brave for me. I will not have your father go troubled to his grave."

"Yes, Mama."

"And, Richard —"

I turned back.

"Yes, Mama?"

She took my hands in hers, and squeezed them. "No tears, my dearest. Your poor father has seen enough of tears."

"Yes, Mama."

No tears! I would have found obedience easier that morning if I had known how many tears I was to shed after that day. How many nights my pillow would become a flood. How many cloudless afternoons I was to water with my private showers. Show me the child who reaches for the hand of father or mother and says "Farewell," and I will show you a storm of weeping under a face of stone.

"There's my strong lad," he said. "No tears. I'm glad to see it."

His voice was so weak, so rasping, that I could barely make out his words.

"You must be good to your mother and sister. You are the man of the house now. They will depend on you."

I bent my head nearer the pillow. He took my hand with a grip so feeble that Charlotte could have squeezed my fingers harder.

"Obey your mother's wishes to the letter."

"Yes, Father."

How selfish it would have seemed if I had cried out then: "Mother and Charlotte, yes! But what of *me?*" Then selfish I must be, for I have sat in this cold and lonely tower room for hour after hour, and the thought has come again and again: "But what of me?" I wish my mother well. Of course I do. And I would not harm Charlotte for the world, nor let another try it. But why did my father forget to mention *me?* Does *my* happiness not matter? Do I count for *less?* Am I supposed to nod and smile and be a brave lad forever, while everything changes around me, and everything I loved is different? No, not just different! I will say it: *worse!*

For things *are* worse. Far worse. Sometimes I sit beside my father's grave and run my fingers over the letters of his name cut deep in stone. And suddenly I fear I will go mad and scramble to my feet and stamp and stamp to wake him and tell him all the things that have gone wrong since he was taken from us. Why should he rest in peace while I become practically a stranger in my own house? Guess who makes all rules now! That black, black bat crept up on my mother while she was busy weeping, and trapped her as surely as if he'd thrown a net on her. "Now, Mrs. Harwick, you cannot see the holes in the chapel path for tears. Please take my arm. I'll see you safely home." "Come, my dear Mrs. Harwick. Together we shall pray." Even while Charlotte could still count on her stubby pink fingers the months that had passed since her last fond farewell to her father, Mr. Cragley was pulling his net tighter. "Lilith, your grief lasts longer than the Lord would ask." And, only weeks later, hiding my own tears deep in the shrubbery, I overheard the words that turned this heart of mine to stone:

"Lily, dear. When you are mine . . ."

When you are mine . . . And, yes! Now you would think he really does own my mother. And everything of hers is his as well. It seems that I am his. And so is Charlotte.

"That boy runs wild. I have a mind to tame him. He must in any case be sent to school. And then perhaps his sister, free from his influence, will be less giddy herself."

And what did my mother say? Did she rise to her feet and flash her eyes, and tell him: "Mr. Cragley, you go too far! My Richard may wander freely around the home and gardens in which he has known happier times, but I'll not have him called 'wild.' And as for little Charlotte, her father and myself were proud to raise a child so fond and loving. We did not call her 'giddy,' and I know he would join with me in being grateful if her new father did not do so either."

Is this how my mother defended us? No, it is not. All that my mother did was lower her eyes, or look away, or press her fingers to the throbbing in her temples and beg Lucy for yet another powder "for my poor, aching head." As weeks went by, the rules grew stricter and stricter, till there were days when (but for the kindness of Mr. Digby showing me how to whittle wood into little animals, and Lucy spoiling me with stolen buns) I would have thought my own home more of a prison, even, than that cold corner of hell to which I was sent four days after Christmas.

Mordanger School. If there's a meaner place on earth, I wish it burnt to ashes. In four long years at this Mordanger School, I have learned nothing except how to freeze, and how to starve, and how to be bullied and beaten. I have been robbed of all my precious little tokens from home. And, in its cold corridors, I have learned how to wait for hour after hour for nothing worth the waiting. Truly, I believe that the entire herd of little wooden cows on Charlotte's toy farm owe their existence to all my teachers' gruesome training. After so many cries of "Sit still, boy!" and "Stop that fidgeting!" now, on my short visits home, I cannot sit for a moment with idle fingers.

"Here, Charlotte. Here's another cow."

She took it and blew on it hard, to watch the sawdust fly. And then she marched it over the brow of the huge glossy globe my stepfather has kindly bought me for my birthday, so he can better torment me with cuffs and blows for not being able to point to China in a moment, or tell him instantly whether the Indian Ocean is larger or smaller than the Pacific Sea.

"Charlotte," I begged her. "Give over spinning the globe. Its very rumble turns my stomach to knots."

Her face went wistful.

"Oh, Dickie," she said. "Why must you hate him so?"

"Perhaps," I said to Charlotte, "you would get closer to an answer if you were to ask *him* why he so hates *me*."

Charlotte sighed deeply.

"Mama says that everything he does is for your own good, so you will grow up strong and manly, and be a son of whom they can be proud."

"I'll be no son of his! Not ever!"

Charlotte turned the cow upside down, and inspected its tiny hooves.

"He has been kind enough to me," she whispered.

Now this was brave of Charlotte! In all the time this man has been in our house, she's picked her way between the two of us like someone stepping on stones over a river with water raging on both sides. While I am near, she takes a care never to slip her hand too willingly in his, or chuckle at his poor jokes, or settle at his feet while he is reading by the fire. But I know well enough, from stepping silently past doorways, and moving like a shadow through the house, that when she thinks that I am far away, watching Mr. Digby prune the roses, or helping Lucy shell beans, then she will nestle to his side, and he will stroke her hair, and pet her, call her his "good, dear Charlie" and beg her to run and fetch his pipe, or slippers, or his *London Magazine*.

I could not help myself. I spat the words at Charlotte.

"Easy for you to like him. You have forgotten how things used to be. You have forgotten our father!"

Her little mouth trembled.

"Dickie! I have not!"

"I think you must, if you can stand without a shudder beside the black bat who seeks to take his place."

"Dickie," she wailed at me, "Papa is dead and gone. Why should I treat Mr. Cragley as if he were a murderer when I know it was not him, but a fever, that carried Papa away? Just because life has dealt us one hard blow, there is no reason for us to be unhappy forever."

"Perhaps you would all live out your fairy tale more happily without the black clouds I bring!"

The tears sprang to her eyes.

"Don't say so, Dickie!"

"And if it should be *true?*"

She hurled the little cow in my direction.

"It *isn't* true! Say it's not true!"

I said it wasn't true. I took her hand in mine, and dried her tears, and begged her pardon. But, deep inside, I know that it *is* true. That, without me, the three of them would get on well enough. Mother, I think, would find life much more pleasant without my dark looks and scowling face reminding her each day that I believe she is a traitor to my father's memory. Mr. Cragley would greet my disappearance with pleasure. And as for Charlotte, she would, I am sure, learn to live without me as promptly and easily as she has learned to live without our dear father.

So here I am, ready to lay down my pen and lift my bag. It seems so strange that, in the instant of bending to the floor to pick up a little wooden cow whose leg has snapped, a boy as young as I could make a decision that will change three lives.

But I have done so.

I am leaving home.

Pixie broke off her reading and lifted her head. From Colin's bed had come a sharp intake of breath, and Claudia was blowing her nose on a tissue.

"Go on," said Ralph impatiently. "Carry on with the story."

But Pixie ignored him.

"Are you two all right?"

Colin pretended that she wasn't speaking to him, but Claudia openly wiped away her tears.

"Yes, go on. It's just . . ."

Pixie gave her a look.

"Just what?"

"Nothing." Claudia shook her head. "Go on."

As Pixie was finding her place again, Rob spoke up.

"I wish my sister could be here to listen to this. She's hated The Beard from the day he moved in with us."

"The Beard?"

Pixie wasn't the only one to glance at him curiously. But she was certainly the only one suddenly to turn back to Colin and Claudia.

"I see!" she said suddenly.

She turned on Ralph.

"What about *you*?" she demanded. "Tell us how *you* fit in."

"What do you mean?"

Pixie was grinning now.

"Come on, Ralph." Just as he'd teased her earlier, she teased him back. "You're supposed to be smart. Isn't it obvious? Colin's been listening for once, instead of daydreaming. Claudia's tissue is soaking. And Rob's sister knows exactly how Richard Harwick feels . . ." She made little beckoning gestures with both hands, like Miss O'Dell coaxing the answer out of someone in a math class.

Ralph shook his head, mystified.

"I'll give you another clue." Pixie's eyes were bright. "I had to put two home addresses on my permission form." Again she imitated Miss O'Dell. "Just think it through, step by step." She grinned. "Step by *wicked* step, maybe . . ."

"Of course!" Ralph brought his fist down triumphantly on the bed. "It's just that I didn't think, because none of my stepmothers have ever been wicked."

"*None* of them?"

Everybody stared. But Ralph didn't even notice. He kept on:

"But, yes. You're right. I did write two addresses on the form."

Now it was Claudia's turn to be confused.

"Which form?"

"The permission form," Ralph told her. "I bet Pixie is right. I bet what we have in common is that we all wrote down a second home address."

"And that's the column Miss O'Dell was looking at when she read out our names to take us off the bus?"

"That's right."

Now Claudia pointed to the album in Pixie's hand.

"Does that mean we all have something in common with him as well?"

Ralph shuddered.

"Oh, no," he said. "We all have *two* homes. Richard Harwick only had one."

Pixie flicked over the page.

"I'm not sure he even keeps that one very much longer."

Ralph reached for his drink.

"Go on," he ordered Pixie. "Keep on reading."

"Yes," Colin said. "Go on. And just be sure you don't miss a single word."

Turning to find his sandwich, he missed the looks of sheer astonishment that came his way. Pixie picked up the album. On the next page, the writing became much tidier and easier to read. If even stare-around-the-room, pay-no-attention Colin was so taken up with the story he was determined to hear the end, she'd keep on.

I shall not tire my reader with the details of my flight. Enough to tell you that it is easy to trade a brand-new school suit for old rags, and orphans are two-a-penny down at the docks. When a great ship strains at the tide, and needs a cabin boy, nobody asks the lad who speaks as roughly as a gardener's son, and claims to be Dick Digby, whether his mother knows he's off to sea. And, for the first time in my life, I wished I'd paid more attention to my lessons. If I'd had my stepfather's globe more firmly in my mind back then, I might be better able now to chart for you the oceans I sailed across, the seas I saw, and our strange ports of call. Twice, in the next few years of dazzling sunrises and haunting sunsets, our ship came home. And twice, instead of doing my duty as a son and brother, and marching up to face my stepfather's wrath, my mother's tears, and all my sister's kisses, I stood like a trespasser in the shadow of the lime walk, and watched the house.

House? Did I call it house? It was more like a tomb. For, as I watched, it seemed to me that all the light and life of my old home had drained from its very stones. Of my mother and sister there was no sign at all — not even the shadow of a dress billowing in front of a window. And in this silent mausoleum where now my stepfather would be at home (the perfect resting place for a black bat!), there was no glimpse of him. Lucy, I saw. But she was hurrying across the courtyard huddled and weeping against the wind; and knowing from early childhood her firm belief in ghosts, I dared not step out from the shadow of the trees, for fear of frightening her halfway to death.

And Digby, too. A dozen times he stopped his digging and turned my way. The look on his face was hopeful — disbelieving. But, peering more closely at the dark dell in which I stood, he shook his grizzled head as if to tell himself he was a foolish old man dreaming of better times, and lowered his shoulders to his work.

That was the last time I saw Old Harwick Hall before this very night. I crept away, back to sea, where fortune shone on me even through storms and shipwrecks. Seaman. Midshipman. Captain. I rose as swiftly as if I swarmed a rope. And it was idly sitting at my Captain's table that my eye fell on the small square of print that brought me home.

WE SEEK NEWS OF
RICHARD CLAYTON HARWICK
OF
OLD HARWICK HALL
WHO IS TO WRITE TO
RIDDLE & FLOOK (SOLICITORS)
TO LEARN SOMETHING
TO HIS ADVANTAGE.

To my advantage! Shame on Riddle and Flook! Only such men of dust could think the deaths of three unhappy souls to my advantage! Oh, yes! Now I am owner of Old Harwick Hall. All of these lands are mine. And I am rich. And what's the good of that? My mother died of heartbreak, my stepfather of fury when he first realized that no trick of his could keep the house from me. And, as for my dearest Charlotte! Read, if your tears will let you, this copy of the letter I found waiting for me in my tower room.

My dearest, dearest Richard,

For you are still dearest to me, though you have been so cruel. Better if you had found the courage to stay, and show patience, and take your part in our troubles, not heap on more by vanishing. Things have been hard with all of us since you left. First Mother spent a fortune seeking you, and all of us suffered Mr. Cragley's anger as money slipped steadily away. "What! Yet another costly search! Let the ungrateful boy be lost forever!" "Lilith! Waste more of your dwindling fortune on this folly and I will make you pay for it twice over!"

And so he did. Last year she died (of him too close, and you too far). And, from the day that she was buried, he would not give a penny to look for you. ("Why hunt for such a knave?") It fell to me to keep the search alive. I have no money of my own. And so, last year, upon my sixteenth birthday, I married Charles Devere. I do not love him as I know I should, and he cannot make me happy. But he is prosperous, and he has promised to keep up the search. Riddle and Flook, his solicitors, daily put notices in every paper. (Oh, Richard! Sometimes I think, not to have seen them, you must have fled halfway across the globe, to Alexandria, or Chittagong!)

And perhaps you will never see them. Or this sad letter. But, if you do, take a moment to weep, for this will be the first and only letter you will receive from your loving sister Charlotte. If I should live, I'd not allow a shadow on your homecoming. But if I die in fever of childbirth, as so many do, then Charles will send this letter to our old home, to tell you why you return to cold, cold silence.

Fare you well, brother,
Your devoted,

You cannot read her name for tears. First hers. Then mine. Oh, how I wept last night. And now, as morning breaks, I have to choose whether to stay and face the damage I have done by piling one wrong on another, till all I loved was broken from the strain; or whether to pick up my bags and disappear again, shutting this tower room forever behind me, and leaving it to the spiders in their webs to quarrel whether I was right or wrong.

I spin the globe, and memories of Charlotte fill the room. Daylight creeps over the sill, where the small broken cow stands so forlornly.

Will I go or stay?

"Go *on*."

Pixie laid down the album.

"I can't. That's it."

"That's *it*?"

"Yes. That's where it stops."

"Stops dead? Just like that?"

"Just like that."

She raised the album, to show them.

They sat in silence until Rob said:

"He must have gone, then."

"Picked up his bags, and slipped away," agreed Claudia. "How awful!"

"Not just for *him*," Pixie reminded her sharply. "What about Lucy and Mr. Digby? What do you think happened to them?"

Once again, Colin astonished them by speaking up.

"I guess, like his mother and sister, they just had to keep waiting and hoping," he said. "And, I can tell you, it isn't very nice, just having to keep waiting and hoping."

He spoke with such a depth of feeling that it was obvious he'd had to do too much of both himself.

"It seems to me," said Pixie fiercely after a moment, "that no one should make decisions that will change the lives of everyone around them without thinking about it for a very long time."

"I did once," Claudia said. "I made a decision in the time it took to blink."

"I bet it didn't change everything around you."

Claudia said thoughtfully:

"Not quite as much as if I'd run away to sea. But it certainly did change things."

Ralph stretched above his head and flicked off the light switch. Shadows filled the room.

"Stories don't have to be written," he reminded Claudia. "This is the night for stories. You begin."

CLAUDIA'S STORY
Green Pajamas

*N*ot long ago, my mum and dad split up. I didn't see it coming. I knew that they quarreled a lot. You couldn't miss it. But I didn't think it was anything special. I'd put on my headphones, or turn up the sound on the television, and they always seemed to make up again pretty quickly. One day my mum would be moaning about my dad:

"I'm fed up with the way he spends all his time running that restaurant. We hardly ever see him, and when we do, he's too tired to be pleasant."

But the next day, if I said anything, she'd take a fit.

"Don't talk about Daddy like that, please!"

And then, one day, he was gone. I came home from school, and everything in the house was moved around. My bedroom radio was in the kitchen. My jackets and shoes were spread out more neatly in the downstairs closet because all his coats and boots had disappeared. The frog mug I gave him for his birthday wasn't on its hook. And some of the photos around the house were gone — just ones of me and him.

"What's going on?"

"Nothing," Mum said. "It's just that your father and I aren't getting on very well at the moment, so he's gone to Granny's house while we calm down."

She tried to sound cheerful about it. But I knew it was worse than she was letting on. (Usually, he calms down working at the restaurant, and she calms down on the phone to her sister. No one had ever gone to calm down at Granny's before. And no one had ever taken a radio and boots and photos.)

He came back quite a lot at first. Not to stay. Just for tea (and more arguments). I'm not completely stupid. Sometimes I listened behind doors, and sometimes I switched my headphones up so loudly that they leaked, but didn't put them in my ears properly, so Mum and Dad didn't realize I was eavesdropping as I walked past them and up the stairs to my bedroom. And sometimes I asked the two of them:

"What's going on?"

"Nothing," they kept saying. "Don't worry. It will all be worked out."

Then, suddenly, everything changed. There was a flood of phone calls late one night, and Mum was in a rage, and even Granny (who'd been very busy "not taking sides") had a huge fight with Dad. And that was the first time I heard the name "Stella." Mum spat it down the phone to her sister so hard that I had to write it on a sheet of paper in curly felt-pen letters and stare at it, before it turned back from a swear word to a name again.

And, after that, my dad hardly dared come near the house. (I think he thought Mum might kill him.) Sometimes he phoned to get to talk to me, and from the freezing way Mum went silent the moment she heard his voice, and held the phone away from her as if it were a bad smell, I'd know it was him. To try and stop her looking like that, I'd rush across so fast I'd trip on the rug, or tip over a milk carton, or something stupid, and feel embarrassed when I spoke to him.

"Hello."

"Hello."

"Good day at school?"

"All right."

"Anything happen?"

"Not really."

"What, nothing?"

I'd look over my shoulder. Mum would be busy wiping up the milk I'd spilled, or clattering dishes as if she wasn't listening. But I knew she was.

"Want to come over on Saturday?"

"If you like."

"No," he'd say, getting irritated. "If *you'd* like."

I'd glance at Mum, who was still listening.

"All right."

I'd try not to sound too pleased, so as not to upset Mum. And after I'd put the phone down, I'd realize I wasn't that pleased, anyway. If I went over to Granny's to visit Dad, I'd miss Natasha's party, or going shopping with Shreela, or working on my project with Fran. And Granny's house was boring. No more boring than usual, but boring all the same. There isn't much to do. None of my stuff is there. And Dad just seemed to sink in his armchair, even more bored than me, and ask impossible questions.

"So how are you? OK?"

Or:

"How's Mum?"

What was I supposed to answer? They're always at you to tell the truth, but what was I supposed to say? "No, I'm *not* all right. I *hate* this, and it's stupid! I don't care how much you and Mum quarrel. I don't even care about this mysterious Stella nobody will talk about. I just want things back the way they used to be, with you home first every Wednesday, and all the fuss about what time I had to go to bed, and you forever complaining about me not turning the hot water faucet off properly, and telling me to take more care over my homework. I want you back, picking the bits of mushroom off your pizza and dropping them onto my plate as if they were slices of fried slug. We had a pizza yesterday, Mum and me, and suddenly I missed you so much that I started crying, and Mum said, "Oh, please don't start, I can't *bear* it!" and I threw my slice of pizza on the floor and slammed upstairs, and locked my door on her. And then there was Mum on one side of the door, and me on the other, both of us howling our eyes out because of you. So don't ask me "So how are you? OK?" and "How's Mum?" or I might answer you! Don't even *ask!*"

Claudia broke off. Outside, the wind still whistled through the trees, but, in the room, the silence was palpable. Nobody even breathed.

"Are you still listening?"

Ralph's voice came out of the darkness.

"Don't be so silly, Claudia. Of course we're listening. Just go on."

Dad stayed at Granny's house till after Christmas. It was the first time we'd ever had a separate Christmas, and it was horrid. I had to choose between not having my presents from Dad on the right day, or not opening them in front of him. (He said he didn't mind, but it was obvious he really did.) And then, the day after, I had to go to Granny's. And that was horrid, too. Mum and Dad were icily polite to one another when I was dropped off. And Granny had insisted on saving the big meal for when we were all together, but I was already sick of turkey and Christmas pudding and cake, so I felt terrible, and so did they.

And it was that night that I met Daddy's Stella. She wasn't in the least what I expected. Up till the moment he pointed her out, walking down the street on the other side, I hadn't realized I had a picture of her in my brain at all. But when I saw her — sort of plain and mousy and dressed in a long brown coat — I realized that I'd been thinking all along that she was tall and blonde and glittery, with fluttering eyelashes and lots of makeup. To be quite honest, I think my mum's a whole lot better-looking than Stella, especially when she's dressed to go out. But Stella was smiling and friendly, and she came over at once and said, "Hello, you must be Claudia," and started asking all that stuff about whether I'd had a nice Christmas, and what presents I'd been given, and how much longer I had off school.

"Were you going anywhere special? Come for a walk with us," Dad said to her in a stagey, false way that made it obvious they'd fixed this whole little accidental meeting up between them. (They'd probably even synchronized watches.) And I was furious, because I hate being treated as if I'm an idiot, and can't work out what's going on behind my back. So I said nothing, and stared down at my feet. And I stopped answering her questions, since I was so annoyed. Dad walked on one side of me, and she walked on the other (though I expect they'd have preferred to be arm in arm). And she kept talking brightly while I marched along as fast as I could, to make it clear I wanted the whole business over as soon as possible. I had to listen a bit, so I could answer "Yes" or "No" whenever she asked me a question. But most of the time I kept my head down and my eyes half-closed, to make the frost on the pavement glitter and dance.

And, in the end, Stella gave up.

"I ought to be getting back now."

"Good-bye," I said, which was extremely rude because, as far as I could make out, we were miles from anywhere. Dad gave me a little dig in the ribs, to remind me of my manners; and I gave him a really vicious poke back, and muttered something under my breath.

"*What* did you say?"

But, when he saw my face, he knew better than to make me repeat it. Well, not in front of Stella, anyway.

And she was bright red now, and just staring bravely ahead of her. She walked even faster than I did after that, and practically ran up the steps to her front door.

Then she turned back to face us.

"Good night, Claudia," she said.

That's all.

And I knew then that she'd be seeing him later, to say good night. Either he'd fib to Granny and say he had to go back and check on things at the restaurant, or he'd make some excuse to go out for a while after I was asleep. And I felt cheated, because I'd only been persuaded to come to Granny's house because of him, and somehow, if he was slipping off to see Stella later, it made me sort of second-best, and not important, as if I really didn't matter much, and might just as well have stayed home with Mum, where both of us would have been happier.

And I *hated* him for it. I wouldn't speak to him all the way back. When Granny asked us, "Did you have a nice walk?" I burst out, "*He* did! *I* didn't!" and stormed off to bed. I thought Granny might come up to tuck me in, and tell me not to fret, everything would come out in the wash, and she bet I couldn't even remember what I was worrying about last year, and all the other things she used to say to cheer me up, when I was younger. But she preferred to stay downstairs and have an argument with Dad about his ruining my visit to their house with his impatience, and sneakily dragging me off to meet "that woman" behind her back. If he couldn't be trusted, she told him, maybe he'd better start looking for somewhere else to stay till things were sorted out.

"I suppose you'd like me to go back!" he shouted. "Well, maybe you haven't grasped this yet, but her mother doesn't want me!"

That made me so furious I pulled my fingers out of my ears, scrambled out of bed and rushed to the top of the stairs.

"*Don't call her that!*" I yelled.

Dad came out in the hall and stared up at me.

"Call her *what?*"

"*That!*"

I banged the door so hard the bureau shook. I *hate* it when they say that. "Your father . . ." "Her mother . . ." "Your daughter . . ." As if, just because we're all separated, we don't even remember one another's *names* any longer!

Next day, my dad moved out of Granny's house, straight in with Stella. Mum was as shocked as I was when she heard. But he made a point of telling her, next time he came to fetch me, that he had nowhere else to go. With the restaurant doing so badly, how could he afford to pay rent while he was still coughing up for us in our house?

"Maybe the restaurant would do a bit better if you spent more time there."

"That's right!" he jeered at Mum. "Have it both ways! For years I'm there too much. Then, when it suits you, I'm not there enough!"

Mum opened the door and stood in silence, waiting for him to leave.

"All right, then," he said. "I'll come around for the rest of my things tomorrow."

"Just tell me when," said Mum. "So I can make sure I'll be safely out."

And that's how we went on for quite a while, with them hardly speaking to one another, and taking turns to come to things at school, and giving me frosty little notes to pass on about things like missing socks and library books. Stella stayed out of it as much as she could. On Wednesdays, when I came for tea with Dad, she used to work late. And on weekends, if I was there, she spent hours reading in the bedroom, and the rest of the time keeping busy in the kitchen. She only sat with us during the meals.

And those were awful. (I don't mean the food. That was excellent. Dad doesn't run a restaurant for nothing, and Stella's a good cook.) I mean the conversation. Stella would try.

"How's everything at school?"

"Fine," I'd say coldly.

"Who's your best friend?"

"Shreela," I'd say, just as coldly. And then I'd add: "But I don't get to see her so much anymore, now that I have to come here."

Then Stella would go quiet, and push a forkful of food around her plate.

"How's Natasha?" my dad would ask.

"She's all right," I'd tell him. "She's going on vacation soon, with her mother and father."

I wouldn't say it; but still you'd hear it ringing around the room: "Lucky Natasha!"

"What about Fran?"

"She's very well, thank you."

Stella would try again.

"I don't know Fran, do I?"

And I'd just stare down at my plate with a look on my face that said, plain as day: 'Why should you? You've nothing to do with me. You're not my mother. Why should you know anything at all about my friends?' If I wanted the butter, I'd ask Dad to pass it, even if Stella was closer. And whenever she asked me a question, I'd try to answer it without even looking at her, as if I just happened to be speaking to the air that just happened to be floating invisibly around me.

And all the time, I would be thinking of Mum. That was the problem. I couldn't bear to sit there, having a perfectly normal time with Dad and Stella, while Mum was at home frantically cleaning out the gerbil cage, or rinsing the glass wall-light shades under the faucets, or hosing mud off the steps. I've never known our house so clean and tidy and organized as the months after Mum and Dad split up. Each time I came home, something else had been painted, or mended, or polished. Mum would look up at me as I walked in. But she waited till the sound of Dad's car had faded around the corner before she asked:

"Have a nice time?"

And it was important to be able to say:

"No. Not really. It was boring."

I can't explain why that helped Mum. Or me. But it just did. I felt, if I'd got along with Stella, if I'd just chatted to her while she fixed her silver necklace, or helped her choose bulbs out of the catalogue for her lovely window boxes, or worn the beautiful green pajamas she bought me as a late Christmas present, then things would somehow have been worse for Mum, even if she wasn't there to see us or hear us. I felt, when I came home and Mum asked, "Have a nice time?" if I'd said, "Yes, I enjoyed it," I'd have been doing exactly the same as Dad. I'd have been cheating on her. I'd be as much to blame as him for all the horrid changes I never wanted.

I couldn't blame Stella, though. I did at first. I hated her at first. I thought, if Stella hadn't come along, Dad would have stayed with us. But it was Shreela who put me right on that.

"He could go home whenever he wanted," she told me. "My dad stormed out once. Then he just came back."

"I heard him telling Granny that Mum doesn't want him."

Shreela shrugged.

"We had a bust-up once," she reminded me. "And we're best friends again."

I thought about that for ages. I couldn't remember what the quarrel was about — something to do with partners for dancing. But after our big fight, I wouldn't make up with Shreela and she wouldn't make up with me. She went off with Fran, and I went off with Natasha. I can't remember how we ended up being good friends again. But I remember all those days of not speaking to one another, and looking away in class, and picking different people on our teams, and acting as if neither of us cared in the slightest.

But we were *seven*. Mum is *thirty-four*. And Dad is thirty-*six*.

Thirty-seven on the night of the party. The night when, in less time than it takes to blink, I made my big decision. From the moment I arrived, I could tell there was something special happening. For one thing, my dad was astonished to see me.

"I thought you weren't coming this weekend."

"Mum had to change it around. Granny mixed up the dates for her appointment at the hospital. We left a message at the restaurant."

"Oh. Right." He looked a bit guilty, as if he hadn't been near the restaurant all day. And it was true. The two of them had spent the whole morning shopping, and now the kitchen was piled high with groceries, and they were frantically chopping and stirring and mixing and blending. I helped for a while (till I'd had enough titbits to count as lunch). But then I went into the other room to do some of my homework. It was quite obvious that they'd be cooking all afternoon.

After an hour or so, Stella came in and started cleaning while I pretended that I hadn't noticed her. She did a proper job, moving the furniture, and wiping and polishing until the place sparkled. From time to time, she said something in my direction, but I either grunted as if I was very busy with my work, or acted as if I hadn't heard over the sounds of clattering from the kitchen. Then Stella went to fetch the knives and forks, and sorted them out on the table.

I watched her carefully from behind my hair. As far as I could make out, she was setting for seven.

"Shall I tell you who's coming?" she said to me.

I shrugged, as if I couldn't care at all, and wasn't really listening.

You could see her struggling to get the names right.

"There's Barney and Mary. And George. And someone called Linda who sometimes works in the restaurant."

Dad's friends. And just at that moment he came into the room. I didn't dare keep up the big freeze with Stella, so I said:

"That's only six, and you're setting for seven."

She stopped and looked at me.

"Don't forget yourself."

"But you weren't expecting me."

"No," she agreed cheerfully. "But now you're here, the more the merrier."

I wondered if she'd checked this out with Dad. Left to himself, I knew, he would have packed me off to the bedroom with supper on a tray. So I said stubbornly:

"I think I'd prefer to have mine upstairs, by myself."

She stopped shunting forks around the table.

"Would you? Would you really?"

"Yes," I said firmly. (And it was true.)

"Tucked up in bed in your nightie?"

I nodded, feeling a bit bad because I hadn't realized that she'd noticed I never wore the green pajamas that she'd given me.

"If that's all right with Dad," I said, as if it had really nothing much to do with her.

"It's fine with me," he said. And you could tell he was relieved. (I suppose you don't invite your old friends around to supper to meet your new girlfriend, and want your daughter at the end of the table, staring at the two of you whenever you talk about how you met, and how things are going, and what your plans are for the future.) He loaded my tray with all the things I like, and gave me a giant helping of dessert, and I went off to bed.

"Comfy?" asked Stella, tucking me in as if I were a baby, and setting the tray across my knees.

I nodded, tugging the sheet up over my nightie like a giant napkin.

The doorbell rang.

"Wish me luck," she said. And I realized for the first time that she was nervous. She knew as well as I did that all Dad's friends would be watching her closely, wondering if they would get to like her, trying to work out why Dad had left home for her, and if she'd be a wicked stepmother to me.

I *couldn't* wish her luck. How *could* I? If she was lucky, it made it harder for my dad ever to come back home. So I just pretended that I'd choked on a baby tomato, and couldn't speak.

She knew I was faking, but she didn't push it.

"Come down if you want anything," she told me. "Anything at all."

And off she went, like someone walking bravely to the scaffold.

The bell rang again. And then again. And while I listened to Dad's friends coming in, and following him to the kitchen for their drinks, and getting settled, I suddenly had an idea. I'd hide behind the giant fern on the landing, and eavesdrop through the meal. Then I'd hear everything. With four people sitting asking polite questions like: "What are your plans now?" and "Will you be moving?" and "Are you hoping to marry?" I'd find out everything I wanted to know, and hadn't dared to ask. For weeks and weeks, I'd had the feeling things were just happening to me. Other people decided things, and made them happen, and I was part of them, but I wasn't told anything about it till after. And I was sick of it. It seemed to me that if I could find out about everyone's plans, I'd be a whole lot safer.

I ate every single mouthful on my tray. Then I slipped out of bed, and took the green pajamas out of the package. Perfect. Absolutely perfect. The exact shade of green!

And off I went, crawling so quietly that no one downstairs heard, along to the giant fern. And there I sat, listening to every word.

And there were enough of them. Words, I mean. The meal went on and on. They talked about everything. Cars. Traffic. Weather. If it was boring, then they talked about it. But all the way through, nobody said a word about Mum, or Dad, or me, or Stella. I realized they were taking special care not to say anything that might lead to trouble. On it went. Boring, boring, boring. Insurance. House prices. Beach holidays. I almost would have fallen asleep.

Except I noticed something. No one was talking to Stella. They weren't turning their backs on her, exactly. But they weren't talking to her. Like me, they talked to Dad, or to the air. The time went by, and no one spoke about the lovely food (in case they had to thank Stella). No one admired the beautiful table (in case Stella had set out all the sparkling things). Nobody asked about her job, or her family, or what she thought. They were, I realized, being as loyal to my mum as they could be. They wouldn't, *couldn't*, make friends with Stella.

They just ignored her.

They were just like me.

And I couldn't help it. I felt sorry for her. She'd worked so hard. I'd watched. She'd worked all day to make things nice for them. And they were treating her as if she were some kind of ghost. They smiled at her vaguely when they had to, and answered her questions politely, and passed her the butter.

But, deep at heart, they were ignoring her.

And it was *rude*. Plain *rude*. This may sound strange, but it was only sitting up there on the landing that I could see how very rude it was. And that it wasn't even helping Mum. Mum wasn't there to see it. And anyway, what had gone wrong had nothing to do with Mary and Barney. Or George. Or Linda. It was between my mum and dad. And treating Stella as if she were invisible was never going to solve it. Shreela and I didn't blame Fran and Natasha when we split up. We just blamed one another. That was fair.

And that was the moment when I made my huge decision. I came out from behind the fern, and stood in my pajamas at the top of the stairs, where everyone could see me: a giant walking houseplant.

Then I sailed down.

"What ho!" said Dad. "Come to say hello?"

But I ignored him. I went up to Stella.

She swiveled on her chair to face me.

I looked her in the eye. I used her name.

"Stella," I said. "These are the pajamas you bought me. Aren't they beautiful?"

I swirled around, and made for the stairs again. On the bottom one, I stopped.

"They're gorgeous," I told her. "Thank you."

I ran upstairs.

I didn't bother to eavesdrop more than a few minutes longer. I felt full of food, and sleepy, and somehow I'd stopped worrying quite so much about what people might say while I wasn't listening. As Granny always says, I shouldn't fret, everything will come out in the wash, and I can't even remember what I was worrying about last year. I just stayed long enough to make sure everyone had got the point. And, sure enough, they had. Mary immediately turned to Stella and asked her where she'd found such lovely pajamas. And George said it was terribly clever of Stella to get exactly the right size.

It wasn't much, maybe. But it was a start.

And then, of course, they just got on to shops. Boring in spades. So I went off to bed. But in those last couple of minutes, Stella had tumbled to where I was, and glanced up twice.

And twice she winked at me.

And I winked back.

It wasn't that much. But it was a start.

Pixie was first to speak.

"You should have brought them with you," she said. "The green pajamas."

"I grew out of them," said Claudia. "I grew out of them at least a year ago."

"Your granny was wrong, then," Ralph couldn't help pointing out. "You *can* remember what you were worrying about last year."

Claudia ignored him.

"I cut them into little squares, and now they're part of my new bedcover," she told Pixie. "Stella's been teaching me how to quilt. She's shown me lots of things. How to read maps and change electric plugs, and how to skate and —"

Colin raised his head.

"Where do you skate?" he asked her.

Claudia stared at him.

"The same place as you."

Colin looked mystified.

"How do you know?"

"I've *seen* you," said Claudia. "I see you there almost every time I go. But you skate earlier, because by the time I arrive, you're always just sitting on one of the benches."

"Are you a good skater?" Rob asked Colin, curious.

Colin went scarlet.

"Not really," he mumbled.

"You ought to be *wonderful*," said Claudia. "You're always there. Can you do backward jumps?"

"Not very well."

He was still looking horribly embarrassed.

"Can you do butterfly halves?" Ralph asked him suddenly, staring intently.

Rob leaned forward.

"Ralph, there's —"

But Ralph cut him off.

"Let Colin answer."

So Colin answered.

"No. Not very well."

"I'm not surprised," said Rob. "There's no such thing."

Colin's flush deepened, and he turned on Ralph.

"That wasn't very nice. Tricking me."

"What I don't understand," said Ralph, "is why you bother to go to the rink all the time if you don't even skate."

Pixie said merrily:

"Is it a story? If it's a story, then you have to tell."

"Yes," Claudia insisted. "I told my story. Now it's time for yours."

"It isn't a story," said Colin. But they were all sitting cross-legged on their beds, staring at him as if it were.

So, cornered, he began to tell.

COLIN'S STORY

The Bluebird of Happiness

*H*is face looked peakier than usual in the moonlight.

"I never knew my real father," he told them. "Mum left him a few weeks after I was born. She says he was a bit of a rough-house and we were much safer away from him, so I'm not sorry about that."

He stretched out his fingers on the quilt, where they gleamed palely like short little rivulets of spilled milk.

"Then she took up with my dad. I call him that because he came when I was eight months old, and I don't remember any time before that. He looks a bit like me, anyway. His hair is dark, like mine, though he has silver patches over his ears. He knows the words of practically every song you've ever heard, and he rolls his own cigarettes out of tobacco in a tin. And he can't sit on a park bench without every dog in the world coming up to say hello to him. Sometimes they even try to follow him home."

He turned his thin face toward the flat silver light pouring through the turret window.

"I call him Dad, but he has about a billion names for me. Col. Collie. Sonny-boy. Buster. Mr. Blue-bird —"

"Why Mr. Bluebird?" Ralph asked.

"I don't know."

"Haven't you ever asked him?"

"No."

"Ssh!" Claudia scolded Ralph. "My granny says 'The child who is loved has many names.' Let Colin get on with his story."

"It isn't a story," said Colin. "There isn't anything to tell. We just went on. My mum worked in a shop, so it was Dad who walked me to school and back. He got my tea, and took me to the park. I used to swing as high as the bar, then lean over so far backward that, when I swung down again, my hair brushed the wood-chips, and all the clouds rolled underneath my feet.

"'Who do you think you are?' he used to tease me. 'The Bluebird of Happiness?'

"And then he'd roll one last cigarette, and we'd set off for home, shooing the dogs off behind us as we went."

Colin fell silent. Everyone gave him a moment, then Claudia said:

"And then?"

"And then," said Colin. "My mum and I did a flit."

"A *what?*"

"A flit," said Colin. "We moved away."

"Why?"

"I don't know. She never really explained. If I went on at her, she'd talk about Dad never bothering to get a proper job, and there being more to life than sitting around singing, and smoking roll-ups. But that was only afterward. She didn't say a word before. She just waited for the one day a month when Dad used to go and spend the day with his sister, and then these two friends of hers came around with a van, and took almost all the furniture and all my clothes and toys, and we went off. I didn't even realize Dad wasn't coming with us. I saw Mum piling his clothes and tapes and stuff into the middle of one of the empty rooms, and still it never struck me. I was so sure he'd be along later that I picked up a tobacco tin that had rolled away into a corner and stuffed it in my pocket, and later, in the van, I asked my mum:

"'Who's going to have the apartment after us?'

"And one of the men helping her snorted and said, 'Well, not Jack, anyway, unless he finds himself a job pretty fast.'

"And Mum said, '*Ssh!*' to him, and gave me a funny little sideways look. Then the van swung around the next bend, and I saw this huge sign saying MOTOR-WAY NORTH, and suddenly I felt sick.

"'Where are we going?'

"'Somewhere nice,' Mum said.

"But she was wrong. It wasn't nice for me. For one thing, I had to start at another school, where everyone had friends already. Nobody bothered with me, except to snicker when I didn't understand all the stuff they'd been doing. Then Mum found a job in a café, and when she came home she was always too busy doing things like making toast and finding clothes for the next day to listen to anything I said about school, and too tired to talk about much herself, except how the noise in the café had given her a headache, and how much her legs ached from being on her feet all day. It wasn't how it used to be with Dad. The thing about Dad is, you can *talk* to him. And he remembers what you say. He'd know the names of all my friends, and if I'd quarreled with them. He knew my favorite animals, and what I'd call my dog if I had one. He knew which teachers I liked, and which I didn't, and what size batteries went in my favorite games, and what I worried about sometimes late at night, and which jokes he couldn't tell me because he had heard them from me in the first place."

"He sounds really nice," Pixie said dreamily.

"He *is* really nice," said Colin. "He's my *dad*."

"Stepdad, really," Ralph couldn't help correcting him.

"*Dad*," Colin said stubbornly.

"Go on with the story, Colin," said Claudia. There was a hint of warning in her voice, but it was clear to everyone that this was meant for Ralph, not for Colin.

"There isn't a story," said Colin. "I just kept at her. 'When's Dad coming?' 'When will he be here?' 'Will he be here for my birthday?' And she always came out with the same old things. 'Soon.' 'When he's ready.' 'When he can.' But I knew there was something wrong, because she said other things, too. 'It was all right for you,' she kept telling me. 'You only saw his good side. You didn't know the half of it.' Things like that. Then she'd go on about him never having a proper job. And if I stuck up for him, she'd just get crosser and crosser. So I shut up."

His black eyes glittered as he turned his face away.

"And I was stupid," he said. "Really *stupid*. It took me ages to realize he wasn't following, and ages more to work out why. He couldn't. Mum hadn't left him any clues. But one day I padded into the kitchen in my socks, and heard her on the phone. 'Just keep your beak buttoned,' she was telling someone. Then she looked up and saw me. And I knew."

He turned back, his dark hair glimmering silver in the moonlight.

"And then I realized it was up to me."

"What did you do?" asked Pixie.

"I wrote a letter." He paused, inspecting his fingers on the quilt. "It must have been dreadful. My writing's bad enough now, but it was even worse back then. And there was no one I could ask for help, because it had to be secret. I didn't dare tell Mum, in case —"

He broke off.

"In case she was furious with you," Pixie suggested.

But it was Claudia who guessed.

"No," she corrected Pixie. "In case she offered to mail it, and then threw it away."

Colin busied himself with a loose thread on his pajama sleeve.

"It didn't matter, anyway," he said defensively. "There was no answer. He must have left the apartment ages before. Maybe it was empty, and the letter just lay on the doormat. Or maybe the family who moved in after us just weren't the kind to bother with other people's letters."

"Listen," said Rob. "He can't just have *disappeared*. He was your *dad*."

"*Step*dad," Ralph repeated.

"*Dad*," Colin corrected him again. "And you don't understand. It wasn't *him* who disappeared. It was *us*."

"But, surely, when your mum realized how upset —"

Rob broke off. Colin was glaring at him.

"Listen," he said. "She didn't *mean* it to turn out like this. It's just that, because she'd had to run away before, to stay safe, she thought it was *better* that way." He turned back to the window and stared out across the moonbleached lawns. "And I did try to explain. I tried a lot. But in the end she'd just get cross with me. She couldn't help it. 'Well, he's not with us anymore,' she'd say. 'So that's that. And one day you'll understand it's for the best.'"

Pixie was scornful.

"Her best, maybe. Not yours."

But Colin just went on staring out into the night, as though pretending that he hadn't heard.

Pixie persisted.

"I mean, to pack him off in a puff of smoke like that! Your own dad!"

"*Step*dad," corrected Ralph, for the third time. And when Colin failed to turn around and argue, he went a little further. "Not even stepdad, really. Unless they were married. Or he'd gone to the trouble of adopting you."

Still Colin kept his back turned.

"What I don't understand," Pixie said stubbornly, "is why just because his mother had finished with Colin's dad, Colin had to finish with him, too."

Colin spun around.

"I never finished with him! It wasn't *like* that! You don't *know*."

"You said —"

Claudia gave Pixie's bedrail a sharp tap.

"Ssh!" she said sternly. "Just let Colin *explain*. Let him get on with his *story*."

"There *isn't* a story," said Colin. "We just went on." He glared at Pixie. "But I hadn't finished with him. I'd —" He stopped. "What I did —"

He spread his hands, stared down at them, and tried again.

"I didn't finish with him. I *pretended*. Each night I took the tobacco tin out of the toe of my boot, where I kept it hidden, and put it under my pillow. Then, very softly, so Mum wouldn't hear, I'd hum our favorite song. And, when I was ready, I unscrewed the lid. There were only a few old shreds of tobacco in there, but still —"

Again he stopped, and glanced around at them. They were all staring back. Claudia was even biting her lip. But no one was laughing at him.

So, bravely, he went on.

"But still, it smelled the same. It was like burying your head in his sweater. Or squashing up in the chair, to watch TV. And I'd pretend that he was there with me. And I could talk to him, just like before."

He took a deep breath.

"I stayed awake for hours and hours and hours, talking to him, although he wasn't there."

Pale silver tears spilled from his eyes and splashed on the quilt.

"I pretend like that sometimes," Claudia comforted him.

"Everyone does," Ralph said impatiently. "Get on with the story, Colin."

But Colin had been distracted.

"Do they?" He brushed the tears from his cheeks, and turned to Pixie. "Do they? Do you?"

"Of course I do," Pixie told him. "Ralph's right. Everyone does it."

Colin turned to Rob.

"What about you? Do you do it?"

Rob was clearly deeply embarrassed.

"Not with my dad."

"But you do it?"

Rob hesitated.

"Of course he does it," Ralph said irritably. "Stop wasting time, Colin. Just get on with the story."

"I've told you," said Colin. "There *isn't* any story. It's just that, as we went on, I started getting into trouble at school from being half asleep. I was sent to see someone because I was doing so badly. But she said there was nothing at all wrong with my brains, and someone else would have to deal with me. So this man came around and talked to Mum, and Mum agreed that I was a bit upset at first, after the move, but I had soon got over it."

"Oh, yes!" scoffed Pixie.

"Settled down in no time!" Ralph echoed scornfully.

"Almost forgotten how things were before," Rob muttered in turn.

"Perfectly happy now," sighed Claudia.

"I'm sure she didn't *mean* to tell lies." Colin defended his mother. "It's just that what she said wasn't the truth. This man sat through three cups of coffee, and Mum didn't even tell him about Dad. Once, when he asked, she just pretended that he meant the other one. 'Oh,' she said. 'Colin hasn't seen his father since he was a baby.' I was standing there listening. And that's what she said."

"And what did *you* say?" asked Rob.

Colin shifted uneasily.

"It was difficult," he told them. "You see, the thing about my mum —"

He took a deep breath, and tried again.

"Don't get me wrong. I love her, and everything. It's just that sometimes I get the feeling that Mum thinks the things that are happening to both of us are only really happening to her. As if how I feel doesn't matter quite so much."

Pixie reached under her pillow and drew out the album. Holding it up to catch the shaft of pale light pouring over the window ledge, she rustled backward through the pages.

"*But what of me?*" she read aloud again. "*I wish my mother well. Of course I do. . . . Does* my *happiness not matter? Do I count for* less? *Am I supposed to nod and smile and be a brave lad forever, while everything changes around me, and everything I loved is different? No, not just different. I will say it —*"

But it was Colin who said it.

"*Worse!*"

They sat in silence, until Rob said:

"Some things don't change much, do they?"

Ralph waved the observation away.

"Go on," he said to Colin. "What happened then?"

"Nothing happened," said Colin. "I keep telling you. It isn't a story. Mum and I just went on, except that one day I came home from school and Mum had thrown away my boots."

Pixie was horrified.

"With the tobacco tin? How could she *do* that?"

"It wasn't her fault," Colin said. "I'd had them for years, and they were far too small. She didn't know that there was something hidden in the toe."

"Couldn't you *tell* her? Couldn't you get them back?"

"You don't understand," said Colin. "It was a secret, the tobacco tin. I don't think she'd have liked it if she'd known." He walked his fingers through the strip of moonlight falling across the bed. "And it didn't make any difference. I still lay awake for hours every night. I was still hopeless in school." He walked his fingers back. "I still am, even at this school. I still get in trouble with teachers. Everyone always seems to be at me. Even my mum. But what's the point in trying to explain how you feel? You know what happens. Everyone acts as if they're listening properly; but really all they're doing is softening you up, so you'll listen to what they're planning to say to you after. And that's always: 'Well, Colin, that's how things are now and I'm sure you'll soon get used to it.'"

His dark eyes flashed.

"But I haven't got used to it! And I never will! I think about him every single day. I try to get on with school and everything, but it's like something waiting around a corner. It keeps rushing out and hitting me. I hear the name 'Jack,' or walk past someone in a jacket just like his. Or I'll be buying gum and see the cigarette papers he used to buy."

He lifted his chin defensively.

"Last week I saw a birthday card he'd really like. It was a picture of a man being followed by a gang of scruffy dogs. I took it off the shelf, and carried it around the shop for ages."

Everyone waited.

"Then I put it back."

"Colin," said Pixie, after a few uneasy moments, "how long is it since you've seen him?"

Colin turned to the window.

"Five years."

"Five *years?*"

He kept his back to them.

"Five years, eight months and seven days," he said.

Flattening his palms on the sill, he leaned forward till his forehead touched the glass.

"I think Mum thinks that I've forgotten him," he told them. "I never mention him at home. But even though I know he can't still be living there, I always secretly sneak his name and our old address on all the forms that Mum's filled in for school, to show he still matters and he's still my dad."

He stood a little straighter.

"But I never talk about him to her anymore. Never. It's part of my plan. You see, I'm saving up now. I save a lot. I keep practically every penny that comes my way. I even do three paper routes. And I keep the money safe, somewhere a whole lot safer than in my boots. And one day soon, I'm going to have enough."

"Enough?"

"Enough to go back and find him."

He turned. With the moonlight behind him, the shadows fell more deeply on his face, making him look years older.

"As soon as I'm tall enough, I'm off. There's no point trying yet. They'd only fetch me back, and it would lead to trouble. So I'm just waiting now. Waiting and hoping."

"And listening to the music down at the rink," said Claudia.

He grinned.

"Mum thinks I'm mad," he said. "She doesn't understand at all. She asks me every birthday and every Christmas. 'Wouldn't you like a cassette player? Wouldn't you even like a radio?' But I always say no, and take the money. And it sounds better, anyway, down at the rink. They play it loud. It bounces off the walls. It sounds so strong and cheerful, so like him, that when I shut my eyes, I can believe that he is still out there somewhere, sitting on a park bench, rolling his cigarettes and singing at the top of his voice."

He turned to the window again, and started humming softly.

"Go on," said Claudia. "Sing the words."

Colin broke off humming long enough to say:

"I'm saving the words till I find him."

"What words?" Ralph demanded of Claudia. "Words to what?"

"Their favorite song," said Claudia. "*The Bluebird of Happiness*. It's on the skating rink's tape, and comes around every hour or so."

The humming stopped again.

"Every forty-five minutes," Colin corrected her, before picking up the tune where he left off.

Claudia ignored him.

"It's about following the bluebird around the world, but finding happiness where you began."

They listened till the end. Then Rob said:

"I'm sure you'll find him, Colin. It's like one of those stories where you just have to keep going to reach the happy ending."

"Fingers crossed," Ralph said.

The others echoed him. "Fingers crossed."

"And there you'll be," Rob finished up triumphantly. "Together again, you and your dad! End of story!"

And in the general passing around and unwrapping of sandwiches which then took place, only Claudia noticed that, this time, Ralph hadn't argued that Colin's father was a *step*dad, and Colin had forgotten to insist that the tale he had told was not really a story.

RALPH'S STORY

A Tale of Three Stepmothers

Ralph reached above his head to switch on the light. "Mine's not a tale of woe," he said, peeling the top slice of bread back from his sandwich to peer suspiciously at the filling. "But it is *complicated,* so you have to pay attention." He laid down his sandwich and started to count on his fingers. "I have two brothers, two half-brothers, one half-sister, three stepbrothers, one stepsister, three stepmothers — that's two old ones and one at the moment — one stepfather, two stepgrannies and one stepgrandpa that I know, and some more that I don't know. And, any day now, when Flora has her baby, I'm going to have another half-sister."

He paused, looking puzzled, as if he'd surprised himself by ending up on the wrong finger.

"Oh, yes!" he said. "And I have a mum and dad."

Satisfied, he went on.

"On Mondays and Thursdays I go directly to Dad's place after school. And every other weekend Mum drives me there, unless it's the third Saturday in the month, when she has her hair trimmed. On that day my stepdad drives me. He's called Howard."

He looked around, as if to check they were still paying attention.

"On Tuesdays, Wednesdays and Fridays, on the other hand, I go straight home to Mum's, unless my dad can't manage the following weekend (if it's his). Then I'm supposed to go to his house to make up, unless it's Wednesday. You see, I have orchestra on Thursday morning, and my horn's never at Dad's house unless we're close to a concert, with Sunday rehearsals, and I was at Dad's house on the Sunday before."

"Stop there," said Pixie. "I'm already lost."

"How can you ever remember where you're going?" demanded Claudia. "You'd have to be a genius to work it out."

"I used to get it wrong a lot," Ralph told them cheerfully. "I'd keep arriving at one house or the other and find no one there. I wouldn't know whether to sit on the doorstep and wait, or go back to the other house. But then they bought me new lunchboxes: two with Mickey Mouse on the side, and two more with Dumbo."

"How did that help?"

"Easy," Ralph said. "*D* for Dumbo and Dad, and *M* for Mickey and Mum. If I wasn't sure which house I was aiming for, I looked at my lunchbox."

"Why *four*?"

"A pair for each house," said Ralph. "And even then they'd sometimes both end up in the same place, and Mum or Annabel would have to stick a label on the side, saying 'Not Mickey, Dumbo,' or 'Not Dumbo, Mickey.'"

"Is Annabel your stepmum?"

"She *was*," said Ralph. "She isn't now. I don't see Annabel anymore. But I still see Angus and Patricia —"

"Angus and Patricia?"

"My ex-stepgranny and grandpa."

"That's it," said Pixie firmly. "I'm giving up."

Ralph stared at her.

"For heaven's sake!" he said. "You can't be lost already. I've hardly *started* to explain."

Claudia patted his hand.

"Don't try and *explain*," she said peaceably. "Just tell us the good parts."

"That's right." Rob backed Claudia up hastily. "Edited highlights only."

Ralph twisted his face up, thinking.

"Okay," he said. "Coming up. One of the best moments ever. This was with Annabel, Stepmother Number One."

He noticed them staring.

"That's what Howard calls her," he explained.

"Who is Howard?" Pixie inquired of the air floating around her. "Do we know?"

"I told you!" Ralph was outraged. "Howard's my stepdad, married to my mum."

A shadow of confusion crossed his face.

"Have I mentioned Felicia, Alicia and Victor?"

"Let me guess," Rob said. "They're your stepsisters and brother."

"*Half*-sisters and brother," Ralph corrected him. "We all have the same mum. My *step*brothers and sister belong to Janet."

"Janet?"

"Stepmother Number Two."

Rob raised both arms, like a referee trying to halt play.

"Go back," he ordered Ralph. "Go back and start again. Don't tell us *anybody's* name unless you must."

"Right."

Ralph began again.

"Me and my real brothers —"

He hesitated.

"Oh, all *right*," sighed Rob.

"Edward and George," said Ralph. "We all went around to Dad and Annabel."

"Stepmother Number One!"

"My brothers were a bit fed up," said Ralph. "They didn't really like Annabel." Again he hesitated. "No, that's not fair. They liked her well enough. She was good fun, and she bought super presents. It's just that she got on their nerves. The problem was that she never left any of us alone with Dad. She was always there. *Always*. She came on every trip, even the boring ones like shopping or getting gas. She sat through every meal, and every TV program. She even tagged along when Dad drove us back to Mum's house. I didn't mind. I was so little that I hardly noticed. But Edward and George just hated it. They said it wasn't fair. She had Dad to herself for half the week, so why couldn't she back off a little bit when it was our time? '*Dad* might have chosen to have Annabel around all day every day,' George complained to Mum. '*I* didn't, did I? Neither did Edward or Ralph. So why do we have to put up with her every single minute?'"

A look of sheer amazement spread over Colin's face.

"He said *that*? To your *mum*?"

Ralph picked his words carefully.

"I don't think my mum comes out of the same box as your mum," he said to Colin. "You can say practically anything to my mum."

He paused a little ruefully.

"And she can say practically anything back. And she did this time. She nagged and nagged at Dad, over the phone. But it was no use. He went on as usual, letting his precious Annabel muscle in on everything, rather than risk the fuss of explaining how George and Edward felt. 'Spineless,' my mother called him. But I think the problem was that he was in love. Totally, idiotically, soppily in love. He and Annabel spent all their time kissing and cuddling and giggling, and calling each other 'Munchkin' and 'Pusscat.'"

"*Munchkin?*"

"*Pusscat?*"

Everyone looked suitably disgusted.

"He didn't seem to *notice,*" Ralph explained. "Everything Annabel did was fine with him. She didn't like jazz, so he stopped listening to it. She thought store bread was stuffed with chemicals, so even if there was nothing in the breadbox, we had to wait for hours, starving to death, while she made more of her own, instead of nipping up to the corner store." He shook his head. "Annabel was always on a dict," he explained. "And, to be honest, I don't think she had the faintest idea how much a normal person *eats*. And she disapproved of coffee, so we all had to drink dandelion tea." He shuddered at the memory. "Dandelion tea! And, every morning, Annabel read her star sign forecast out loud, and then she read it again in the evening, explaining how you could look at it so it was almost right. And Dad didn't even *laugh* at her! And Annabel believed that everyone had an aura around their head, a sort of ring of color that shows what kind of person you are, and what sort of mood you're in. Nobody else can see auras, but Annabel claimed she could. Sometimes, she'd look at Edward or George and say, 'Your aura's looking very thin and gray. Did you have a bad day at school?' And even if they'd had a simply dreadful time from start to finish, they'd force themselves to say, 'No, it was great,' just to embarrass her in front of Dad." He shook his head in wonder. "Except that Dad wasn't embarrassed. He'd just beam. 'Cracked,' said my mother. But I think it was just that he was dippy in love. Until the day —"

He broke off. A seraphic smile spread over his face. "Go on!" they scolded him. "Get on with it."

"Until the day we had to bring Brandy with us."

"Brandy?"

"Our cat. He couldn't stay home, you see, because Mum was varnishing floors. 'I'm not packing you three off to your Dad's, and Felicia out in the stroller with Howard, just to have that fat, idle, inconsiderate pet of yours leave paw prints down my freshly varnished hall, so he'll just have to go with you. And if your dad makes a fuss, tell him from me he's lucky I don't send Brandy every week,' she said."

Colin looked suitably impressed.

"You're right. Your mum can say *anything*."

Ralph winced.

"We don't pass all of it on," he admitted. "We didn't that time. We just rolled up, with Brandy squashed in a cage Edward had put together from a broken milk bottle crate and pieces of wire. And Annabel went on about how *cruel* we were, *poor* little Brandy, hardly room to *breathe,* till Dad distracted her by pointing out that we were out of bread again. 'Shall I send Edward to the store?' But no! Annabel insisted on making it herself. So we sat around the kitchen, starving to death, while Annabel fussed with yeast, and kneaded, and sang her 'lucky chant' over the dough, then put it in the big brown china bowl to rise."

Again the seraphic smile suffused his face.

"And Edward said, 'Come on, George. Let's go out. We'll take Ralph with us.' And we went to the store, where Edward spent his whole allowance on three large loaves, and we ate all of them on the way home. Then George and Edward brushed the crumbs off me, and we went back inside."

The light of joy shone in his eyes.

"Annabel's dough had risen miles high," he said. "It was a huge, puffy ball, bulging up out of the bowl. '*See?*' Annabel told us. 'Isn't it worth the wait?' She turned to get her baking tins out of the cupboard. And just at that moment Brandy leaped up on the table and sniffed the dough. Then he lifted a paw and patted it, terribly gently."

Ralph's grin was rapturous.

"And George looked at Edward. Edward looked at George. And George put his hand over my mouth, so I couldn't say anything."

He wriggled in ecstasy.

"And, just at that moment, Dad came in the room. So we were all there to watch as Annabel turned around in time to see our fat old Brandy curling himself up comfortably on her dough, and blinking coolly at her over the edge of the bowl while it sank like a parachute beneath him."

He rocked on the bed in his rapture.

"And Annabel went *mad*. Totally unhinged. You've never seen anything like it. She said that Brandy was an evil beast who had spoiled her bread dough out of sheer spite. Dad tried to stick up for Brandy. ('More than he's ever done for you children!' Mum said afterward.) But Annabel wouldn't listen. 'I saw that creature for what he was the moment he came into the house,' she said. 'He has a malevolent aura. Look at the purple ring around his head.'"

Ralph spread his hands.

"And that was that," he said. "Dad burst out laughing. He just couldn't help it. 'Malevolent aura!' he scoffed. 'Our Brandy? Purple ring around his head! Don't be *ridiculous,* Annabel!' Then he shooed Edward and George and me out of the room, so they could go on without us listening. But we didn't need to hear anymore, really. The spell was broken, it was obvious. And though they kept calling one another 'Pusscat' and 'Munchkin' for quite a bit longer, in the end Annabel ran off with someone who thought he was a descendant of King Arthur, and it took Dad ages to find her to get her to sign the papers for the divorce."

"Where is she now?" asked Colin.

Ralph only shrugged.

"Don't you know?" Colin asked, adding, astonished: "Don't you mind? Don't you miss her?"

"No," Ralph said. "I can't say I mind. I can't say I even missed her. You see, she was more of a girlfriend of Dad's than a real stepmother. And anyway, right after she went off, Dad took up with Janet, and that took all my attention for a while."

Rob settled himself more comfortably.

"Is this another highlight coming up?"

Ralph gave this a moment's thought before admitting:

"I think it would be fairer to call it a few lowlights."

"Go on," said Claudia. "Off you go. Stepmother Number Two."

"She was a real shock," said Ralph. "Not one of us had ever come across anyone like her before. George thought Dad must have found her in a *jail*." He noticed the curious looks on their faces. "Not in a *cell*," he added hastily. "In the main office. Running everything. She was more keen on rules than anyone I've ever known. Janet had rules about everything. Rules about what you could watch on TV, and for how long. Rules about what time everyone had to go to bed, and when they had to get up, even on Saturdays. She even had rules about what sorts of food you were allowed to take out of the fridge without asking. She used to treat a lump of cheese as if it were the crown *jewels*."

He sighed.

"And mealtimes were the worst. Janet had rules about how you had to chew, and what you had to do with your elbows, and how to hold your knife and fork. There was a rule about not sliding the butter dish along like a hockey puck. There were rules about saying 'Please' and 'Thank you' and 'May I pass you the bread?' There was a rule about not starting to eat until everyone at the table had been served. There was a special knife for the butter dish. There was a special spoon for the jam."

He shook his head in renewed amazement.

"And there was even a rule that no one could get up and answer the telephone if it rang unless everyone around the table had finished their dessert."

He scowled.

"I must have missed about a million calls!"

"What about your dad? Didn't he mind?"

"*Mind?*" Ralph said bitterly. "He *liked* it. He said after Annabel it was wonderful. 'Sensible,' he called it. 'Organized.' And everyone else seemed to agree. Edward and George thought she was wonderful because they had tons of time alone with Dad while she was rushing between doctors and dentists and school shows and parents' evenings with Tom and Joe and Doug and Ann."

He noticed their baffled faces.

"My stepbrothers and sister," he explained. "Janet's own children. They moved in as well. 'Giving it a try,' Janet called it." He scowled again. "I could have told them all it wouldn't work. The house wasn't big enough. I didn't mind Tom so much. And Ann was quite nice, once you got to know her. But you'd need a *castle* for me to get along with Joe and Doug. Not that anyone listened to me, of course.

"What did your mum say?"

Ralph made a face.

"That's one of the things I don't understand," he told them. "Mum and Howard thought Janet was wonderful. Maybe it was because she came so quickly after Annabel. But 'It's so nice to have a bit of *order* in our lives for once,' my mum kept saying. 'And to give credit where it's due, I've never seen your clothes come home so beautifully laundered. She even got those oil stains off Edward's shirt. Do you think I dare send her that crib blanket of Alicia's?' My mum spent hours on the phone with her. In fact, she hardly bothered with my dad at all, once Janet came. Anything complicated — dates for holidays, extra rehearsals, exchange visits to France — she just fixed up with Janet. 'What a *joy*,' she kept saying, 'to deal with a woman who can draw up a proper schedule. Let's hope it lasts.'"

"And did it?"

"Oh, yes," said Ralph. "It lasted." He sighed. "I think if anyone ever sends me to prison, I'll know exactly how to behave. I'll pick up the rules in no time. I'll know how to share a tiny cell between three people. I'll know not to leave any of my stuff lying on someone else's patch of floor, in case they trample on my things, and break them. I'll know better than to be more than a microsecond late for any meal because, with so many people in the house, the person who cooked it can't be expected to think about saving things for latecomers. I'll certainly remember to take all my model cars off my bookshelves and lock them away sensibly in my cupboard, where I can't even *look* at them at night. And I won't expect to get to watch what I want on TV more than once in a lifetime."

His voice shook with scorn.

"I'll know to give a year's notice if I want a bath. And not to expect to get more than one measly piece of candy out of a box if I have to share it with everyone. I'll know how to read some very complicated charts about whose turn it is to wash, and dry, and put away, and dust, and sweep the kitchen floor, and wipe down the counters."

His face was scarlet.

"Oh, yes," he said. "I'll be really at home in prison."

Claudia said soothingly:

"But, surely, Janet's gone now."

"Yes," Ralph said, calming down. "Janet's gone now." And at the thought of it, his spirits rose. "She got fed up with Mum and Dad. First she said they were taking advantage of her. Then she said neither of them pulled their weight. And in the end she said that both of them had pushed their luck too far."

"What had they *done?*"

Ralph blushed.

"Well, Dad kept business trips on the days when we were there. 'You've got four anyway,' he kept telling Janet. 'Three more won't make any difference.' And then Mum started sneaking Victor's romper suits into Edward's sports bag, hoping that Janet would come across them and get the stains out before sending them back."

"That's terrible!" said Pixie. "So unfair!"

"My mum's a bit like that," Ralph confessed. "Even Howard said she'd got no more than she deserved, and it would serve her right if Stepmother Number Three sent back our socks and underwear without even bothering to wash them." He grinned. "Mum blamed my dad, of course. And Dad blamed Mum. But nobody else gave a hoot. We were too happy. I could spread all my models along my shelves again. We ate out of pizza boxes and potato chip bags. And George even organized a ceremony for dropping the butter knife down the drain."

He picked up his sandwich again.

"It was like suddenly being set free," he said. "Wonderful. And we went on like that until last year . . ."

"Stepmother Number Three!" they chorused willingly.

"They haven't married yet," said Ralph. "But she's moved in. Her name is Flora." A look they hadn't seen before spread over his face, and he told them disconcertingly, "Flora means Flower," before falling silent.

Claudia prompted him.

"Ralph?"

He seemed not to hear her, so she said it louder.

"Ralph!"

He started.

"What?"

"Tell us. Tell us about Flora."

He flushed.

"Oh, yes. Well, Edward met her first. He dropped in unexpectedly to pick up his school biology project on skin diseases, and found her lying on Dad's patio with hardly any clothes on. Dad looked uncomfortable, and said: 'Edward, this is Flora. Flora, can't you cover yourself up?' And Flora said, 'I'm enjoying the sun. Why don't you cover up Edward?' So Edward put a bag over his head, and they had a nice long chat about leprosy and diaper rash."

"*Very* nice," murmured Pixie. But Ralph didn't seem to notice. He just went on with his story.

"George didn't meet her till the day after that. She came with Dad to pick him up from his viola lesson, and they went shopping for food. George said he'd never seen anything like it. Strawberries, kiwi fruits, waffles, Belgian chocolates. Dad nearly had a fit. He kept coughing anxiously and peering into his wallet. But Flora went on dumping treats into the cart. And when they reached the checkout, Dad tried to make a stand: 'We don't have room in the freezer for four separate ice-cream cartons.' Flora ignored him, George said. But seeing Dad squinting gloomily in his wallet again, the lady at the checkout picked out the chocolate fudge ripple and the toffee pecan, and said to George: 'Be a dear, and put these back for your mother.' Flora nearly dropped a bottle of luxury maple syrup. 'I'm not his mother!' she said. 'I'm *far* too young to be his mother!' And she looked absolutely *horrified*. But nowhere near as horrified as Dad, George said, when he was telling us after. Mum rolled her eyes to heaven, and Howard laughed and said: 'Here comes Stepmother Number Three.' But I felt out of it because I hadn't met her, so I didn't have anything to tell."

"You've met her now, though."

"Oh, yes," said Ralph. "I've met her now."

The strange look drifted back across his face.

"*Well?*" Pixie demanded.

With an effort, he dragged his attention back to them.

"What?" he said.

"Meeting *Flora*," prompted Claudia.

"Oh, yes," said Ralph. "I met her the next day. Mum was sticking to Janet's schedule. 'It's like Annabel's lunchbox trick,' she said. 'Too good to give up just because she's gone.' So I went over to Dad's as usual, and Flora opened the door. 'Hello,' I said. 'Here I am.' And she looked me up and down and said, 'That's very nice, but who are you?'"

He grinned. "It wasn't easy to explain. I started by telling her, 'I'm Ralph.' But since she still looked blank, I thought I ought to add something, and the best I could come up with was, 'I think I might be one of your new sort of stepsons.' She didn't look frightfully pleased, I must say. In fact, she stormed off to the living room, to phone my dad. I heard her through the door, sounding ratty. 'What do you *mean*, you can't get away from work?' I don't know what he said, but it can't have worked any better on Flora than Janet, because the next thing I heard was Flora slamming down the phone. Then she came back.

"'Your dad's got a nerve,' she said. 'I'm not a nanny!'

"'And I'm not a baby,' I snapped. (Well, I was hurt.) And then, to prove it, I went into the kitchen. 'I'm getting myself a cheese sandwich,' I told her. But somehow a little bit of Janet must have stuck, because I couldn't help adding politely: 'May I make you one, too?' She stared for a moment, then snatched up her bag. 'Don't bother making us sandwiches,' she said, as if we were already some sort of team. 'We'll eat out.'

"'But what about Dad?' I asked, and she gave me a bit of a cool look.

"'What *about* him?'"

Ralph grinned. "And I could see her point. If he couldn't even get home in time to introduce us on the day we met, why should we worry about him? So off we went. We had the best time ever. First we had Chinese food. Then she took me to a film about Killer Tomatoes. And then, while we were arguing about aliens on the way home, we bumped into some of her friends and went off to a coffee shop, where I took the chance to sneak away and phone Dad.

"'Where are you?' he squawked at me.

"'We're at the Purple Onion,' I told him. 'We're just having a nightcap with a couple of friends, and then we're on our way home.'

"So, naturally, he went berserk.

"'Do you know what the *time* is?' But I pretended that my money had run out. 'Back soon,' I said. But we weren't, because Flora took her time over her coffee. It was eleven-thirty when we got home. Dad was climbing the walls. 'How could you *do* that?' he said to Flora. 'It's going on midnight. On a school night!' But Flora only pulled out the pins in her hair and tossed her head, and told him cheerfully: 'Oh, well. Another time, maybe, you'll think twice before leaving him in my care without checking about *my* plans.' She shook her hair into the most amazing fan around her face, and winked at me from behind, so he couldn't see."

Again, the vague, bewitched look spread over his face, and he fell silent, staring into space.

"You're totally soft on Flora, aren't you?" Rob said.

Ralph made no effort to deny it. He just sighed.

"I think she's *wonderful,*" he admitted. "She's done all sorts of terrible things to me. She poured a bowl of spaghetti over my head when I was rude to her. She picks me up from school *hours* late. I practically finish my homework sitting in the gutter. She gets me in trouble, sneaking me into films I'm not old enough to see, and places I shouldn't go. If I complain, she only says, 'Don't moan at me. I'm not your mother!' She's completely disorganized. She bought me the most amazing stone frog in the January sales, and then forgot my birthday. And now she's pregnant, she's impossible. Yesterday, she sent me *miles* to buy a bottle of mint sauce for her sandwiches."

"Mint *sauce?* For a *sandwich?*"

"That's all she eats now," Ralph told them mournfully. "Mint sauce sandwiches. I worry about this baby. She'll never look after it right. All the responsibility will fall on me. Mum says if Flora craves mint sauce, it's because her body needs it, and I should stop fussing around her like an old hen. But in all the baby books —"

"You're not reading baby books!"

Rob was aghast.

Ralph stared.

"Of *course* I am. This baby is my *sister*." Noticing Colin's eye on him, he corrected himself with an effort. "All right, then. Half-sister. Or half-*brother,* maybe. But either way Flora's not going to be much use. All she's ever looked after in her whole life is a goldfish. And that was found floating belly-up in its bowl."

He squared his shoulders.

"No, I'm afraid it's up to me. But Mum has promised I can spend a bit more time around there, just till I get them better organized."

Pixie asked curiously:

"Doesn't your mother *mind* you being —" she hesitated, trawling for a more delicate way of putting it, and then gave up and copied Rob's phrase — "being totally soft on your stepmother?"

Ralph blushed.

"She teases me about it a little. Everyone does. Yesterday, when I was sorting out the baby clothes that Mum is lending me, George even pointed out that I am actually nearer in age to Flora than Dad is, so if she's going to marry anyone, maybe it should be me."

A huge grin crossed his face.

"But Howard said I should just thank my lucky stars that Stepmother Number Three turned out to be a winner."

"Do you think she'll stay?"

Ralph held up crossed fingers.

"She's settling down," he said judiciously. "No doubt about it. George and Edward keep warning me not to bank on it. It might just be the baby. It might not last. But when I was helping her sort out some old toys and rattles and stuff, she picked up a fairy-tale book she's had since she was four, and started to read. "'*Once upon a time there was a beautiful stepmother who lived with her three wicked stepchildren, deep in the woods . . .*'"

He grinned again.

"I checked it later, and she'd changed it around. But I think, if she can make a joke like that, she must be settling down."

"Oh, yes," said Claudia. "And, after all, it is supposed to be 'third time lucky.'"

"That's what I think," Ralph told them. "At least, that's what I hope."

The soft look came back again, just like before.

"Third time lucky," he said, and held up his fingers, which were crossed again.

Pixie threw herself backward on the bed, tucked her arms under her head, and told the ceiling gloomily:

"If it's third time lucky, I've a long way to go."

Everyone shifted around to face her.

"Well, go on," said Rob. "Tell us."

Pixie sat up again.

"Why? Am I next?"

"I thought we were going around in a circle," said Claudia. "It should be Rob now."

"I don't mind Pixie going first if she's ready."

"Ready?" teased Ralph. "She's probably even worked out a *title*."

"Yes," Pixie told him. "I do have a title. I'm calling my story 'The Pains in My Life.'"

Ralph settled back.

"All right, then. But no fancy frills. We want the truth, and nothing but the truth, or it won't count."

"What makes you think —?"

But since she could already hear them snickering, she thought it safer to begin.

The Pains in My Life

$\mathcal{R}$eally, of course, their name is P - a - y - n - e, but, like me, you'd call them "The Pains" if you met them. They're awful, Sophie and Hetty Payne. They drive me up the wall. I almost don't want to bother seeing my father anymore, now it means that I have to spend weekends at their house. Lucy, their mother, isn't so bad. I can ignore her. She makes a fuss of me when I arrive, and asks the usual questions about school. But, after that, she tends to lose track of me. I used to disappear upstairs, and only come down at mealtimes, or when someone called me. And maybe we would have kept on that way forever, except that Sophie and Hetty had a terrible quarrel a few months ago, a real stand-up fight, and Lucy and Dad decided the sensible thing was to move Hetty out of her sister's bedroom into mine.

Mine!

It was *agreed* when Dad and Lucy bought the house that I'd have a bedroom to myself. I remember that.

Mum remembers it. And even Dad admits that was the deal. No sharing bedrooms with my stepsisters. But then there was this fight. We'd all seen it coming. Sophie and Hetty had been scratching at one another for months.

"Hetty's using my calculator, and she won't give it back to me."

"Sophie keeps switching channels while I'm watching."

"Hetty wore my blue sweater while I was out yesterday, and now there's a hole in it."

"Sophie's sitting on the stairs, and she won't let me past her."

You'd think that they were *three,* the way they went on. And you'd think they'd be used to it. (Everybody else was.) But, no. All of a sudden there was this giant bust-up — fists flying, hair pulled out in chunks, and all Sophie's little glass animals smashed to bits.

So I end up with Hetty. In my room. One Friday I show up and lock myself away in peace and quiet as usual. And on the next visit I can hardly get into the room for Hetty's bed and Hetty's desk and Hetty's chest of drawers.

"What's going on?"

Dad looked at Lucy. Lucy looked at Dad. Then Lucy said:

"We didn't think you'd mind. It's not as if you're here that much. Only a few days a month. And Sophie says she won't share with Hetty any longer."

What could I do? What could I say? I could have tried to argue. I could have said that I'd been promised a room of my own. Everyone had said I wouldn't have to share. But it wouldn't have sounded very nice of me. It would have sounded rather petty and mean (unless I added a bit about not being all that keen on coming anyway, and I couldn't really do that with Dad standing there, could I?).

And Lucy was right. A few days a month isn't much. It wouldn't really have mattered, except that even a day feels like a year if you can't stand the person two feet away from you.

And I can't stand Hetty Payne. I just can't stand her. I'm not too keen on Sophie, to be fair. But Hetty drives me mad. I hate the way she cocks her head on one side and fiddles with her hair. I hate the way she sniffs without noticing whenever she's reading. I even hate the way she rolls the cat over the carpet like a sausage. But most of all I hated the way she teased me about my name.

"Lunchtime, Priscilla!" she'd yodel up the stairs.

And though I wouldn't answer till someone else came along and called up "Pixie!" it still made me want to creep out of my room and drop a heavy pot plant on her head.

And she'd been put in with me. I was supposed to get along with her from Friday after school to Sunday night, on two weekends a month.

"This isn't fair," I grumbled to my dad. "She's Sophie's sister, not mine. Let Sophie put up with her.

Or let her use my room while I'm not there, and move back with Sophie when I come. That would be fine with me."

"Lucy thinks Hetty might find that unsettling," said my dad. "She thinks it's easier this way."

Lucy thinks . . . Lucy thinks . . . But he was my dad before he was Lucy's husband. I'm only here for two weekends a month. Do you think it would kill him to try and stick up for *me* once in a while, instead of crawling around his new family as if everything about them mattered *more?*

But none of them ever seemed to think about me. Nobody even asked. When all of us went to France for the first time, Sophie and I had a fight. We were supposed to be one brand-new, big, happy family, and Sophie took the top bunk bed without even asking me, or tossing a coin. I pulled her stuff off and threw mine up, and she hurled it down again. Then we were thumping each other, and lashing out, and snatching at one another's hair. The tears were streaming down our cheeks, but we never made a noise, not a single peep, in case Dad and Lucy came in from the next room and saw what a terrible mistake they'd made, and how much they were fooling themselves, and how stupid they were to think we would ever feel anything about one another except: "Get out of my *life,* please. Just go *away!*"

And I didn't feel any different about Hetty. In fact, I felt worse. Hetty is nearer my age, but we couldn't be more different. You only have to pin back your ears for half an hour to get your head stuffed to bursting with Hetty's gift for math, and Hetty's natural good manners, and Hetty's way with animals (if you can call rolling a cat across the floor "having a way with animals").

Hetty is everyone's darling. Except mine. When she holds up her homework with its neatly written *"Excellent!"* at the bottom, I want to snatch it from her and rip it up. When she reaches for her helping of dessert and starts with her creepy "Oh, *delicious,* Mum!" I want to push her face in it. And when she leans over to point to all the little mistakes in my math, I want to stab her finger with my pen.

So how to get rid of her, out of my room? First, I tried a haunting. As soon as the light was out on Friday night, I stretched out my arm as far as it would go, and started a scratching, scrabbling noise between the two beds.

"What was that?"

"What?"

"That noise."

"Wasn't it you?"

There was a worried silence. Then she said:

"No, it wasn't me."

"Oh, well," I said cheerfully. "Maybe we're haunted." And left it at that until the next morning when she went off for her shower. As soon as she was out of the room, I flung the window wide open. Luckily, Hetty never hurries in the bathroom. So by the time I heard her coming back and tugged the window closed, the room was icy cold.

"What's going on in here?" she said. "It's *freezing*."

I shrugged.

"Strange thing," I said. "One minute it was fine. Then, just a moment ago — whoosh! It was like the Arctic."

Clutching her towel around her, she went to the radiator.

"Funny. The heat's still on."

"Very odd," I agreed. "I thought this sort of thing only happens when there are ghosts about."

She looked up.

"You don't think —?"

"Here?" I laughed. "There's no reason to think that horrible, horrible murder happened *here*."

"What horrible, horrible murder?"

I stared at her.

"Didn't you know? I thought that everyone knew about Poor Henrietta Forbes. How her husband accidentally locked her in a wardrobe, set fire to it by mistake, and then, without thinking, put the flames out with an axe."

Hetty sat down on her bed.

"I didn't know."

"Her ghost was seen up and down the street for years. But then a priest came, and she was laid to rest. The story I heard was that the spirit of Henrietta Forbes would only walk again when someone with the same name lays their bed, uninvited, in her place."

I finished up cheerfully:

"So you're all right, then."

"No, I'm not!" Hetty snapped.

I spun around, pretending I'd just realized.

"Hetty! Of course! It's short for Henrietta!"

But maybe I'm not as good an actress as I thought, because she suddenly cottoned on, and grinned at me as if I were the cleverest person in the universe, just for thinking up some silly ghost tale. I realized there was no point in carrying on with the haunting. So next day I tried something different to drive her out. Bothering her back. I waited until she was deep in her homework. Then I picked up my math book, littered with all the usual "*Try again, Pixie*"s and "*Please see me*"s, and brought it over to her desk.

"Can you explain things?"

Can Hetty Payne explain things? Can camels *spit?* My stepsister can explain things till hell freezes over. I stood there, bored out of my *mind,* while she went through each problem, and why you have to tackle it the way you do, and where it's easy to go wrong. I got so bored I even started listening (and some of it must have accidentally stuck, because a week later, for the first time in my life, I found a neat little "*Well done!*" on my math test).

But it was still pointless. Hetty didn't even seem to *notice* me wasting hours of her time, let alone *mind.* After, without even moaning, she missed a couple of her favorite TV shows to write her essay, and then got up early next morning to finish her own math.

And that's when I tried the next tack to get her out of my room. The semi-silent treatment.

"Are you coming swimming this afternoon?"

"Maybe."

"Don't you know?"

"Not yet."

"Well, can't you decide?"

"When I'm ready."

I kept it up all morning. I wasn't exactly "not speaking." And I wasn't quite sulking. But I certainly didn't make things easy. I hoped she'd suddenly get so fed up with me that she'd decide even her sister was better company, and sweep her clothes off the end of my closet rail, and storm back to Sophie. I could imagine them discussing me behind my back.

"Mean! Hateful!"

"Selfish! Horrible!"

And I was *almost* right. She left the room. But not to go back to Sophie and crab about me behind my back. Oh, no. Hetty the Pain went straight to her mother, and told her what was going on.

And Lucy showed up in my doorway. She was as mild and friendly as usual; but just from the way she was ready to break off whatever it was she'd been doing to talk to me, I knew she was taking this seriously. It mattered to her.

And suddenly I realized that it was serious to me as well. It mattered even more. I'd gone for months just drifting through my weekends in their house as if they were some sort of halftime in a football game, and real life started again when I went home on Sunday night. I was sick of hiding my feelings. I was sick of holding my tongue. And, most of all, I was sick of pretending.

She'd better be careful, I thought. She'd better watch out. Or this time she'll hear a bit more than she was expecting.

She started off carefully enough. She perched herself neatly on the end of Hetty's bed.

"I hear there's a bit of a problem between you two."

"I don't think so," I said warily.

"Hetty says you're not talking to her."

"I'm talking."

"Not properly, she says."

I turned away.

"Maybe I don't want to talk to Hetty all the time," I said. "After all, I'm not used to sharing a bedroom with someone who isn't family."

"Hetty *is* family."

"No, she's not," I said. "Not to me. Not really."

I turned back and saw that Lucy was suddenly looking very nervous. She hadn't realized I was going to break the rules and say exactly what I thought, for once.

"She is your stepsister," she pointed out.

"Yes," I said. "She's my stepsister. But you and Dad at least got to *choose* one another. You two *decided* that you wanted to live in the same house and share a room. Hetty and I have just been shoved in together. We didn't get to choose. We're just expected to pretend to get along, so it suits everyone else."

Lucy said slowly:

"But don't you think that's true for pretty well everybody in the world? After all, you don't even get to choose your own parents, really, do you? It's only chance."

I couldn't believe it! I could not *believe* it. Here I was, trying to explain how I *feel* about having to share a room with someone I don't really *like,* who isn't even *family*. And Lucy's not even listening! She's sitting there thinking up stupid arguments to try and beat me down!

"That's different!" I snapped at her. "Quite different! And you *know* it!"

She went bright red. She knew that I was furious. Rattled, she tried another tack.

"And I didn't choose you, either," she pointed out. "But I still try to get along with you."

Then, suddenly realizing this might have sounded pretty nasty, she added hastily:

"And your dad didn't choose Sophie or Hetty, either. But he tries to get along with them. We *both* try."

"So you should!" I said rudely. "After all, it was you two who made things turn out this way, not me and Hetty and Sophie."

And then, to spite her, I added:

"Or my mum."

That got her. You could see she was willing herself not to jump up and slap me. And I'm not even sure she would have got a grip of herself in time, except that, just at that moment, the door handle gave a little creak as it began to turn. Both of us saw it. It must unmistakable. I thought at first that it was Hetty the Pain, come back to gloat. But when the door opened a crack, both of us could see from the height of the shadow behind it that it wasn't Hetty at all. It was my dad.

We heard his soft intake of breath.

"Whoops!"

And the door closed again. He'd obviously sensed that there was trouble brewing, and rather than come in and help us sort it out, he'd just decided to stay safely out of things, as usual.

I wasn't in the least surprised. And neither was Lucy. But she was really irritated, you could tell. And past bothering to hide it.

"That's right!" she hissed scornfully at the door. "Sneak away! Leave it all to the Wicked Stepmother, as usual!"

Maybe I should have been more careful. But I was irritated, too. It just popped out.

"Nobody *forced* you to marry him."

She turned on me.

"No," she said icily. "Nobody forced me. And if I'd had the faintest idea what I was getting into, I wouldn't have done it in a million years!"

I was astonished. And I must have showed it, because Lucy added sarcastically:

"No need to look so surprised. When was the last time you heard any of your friends saying they want to be a stepmother when they grow up? Never, that's when. And I can tell you why. Because it's not a life anyone in her right mind would choose!"

"Better than being a stepdaughter," I muttered bitterly. "Or a stepsister."

"Oh, yes?" she said, stung. "Well, I don't think you can claim to have put too much of an effort into being either. You show up here twice a month. You don't take the slightest interest in anyone or anything around you. You sneak up to your bedroom as soon as you reckon you can get away with it, and only bother to come down to eat. I cook your meals for you. I change your sheets. I clean your room. I even wash your clothes. And you never even bother to thank me for any of it."

"You can't have it both ways!" I snapped. "Either I'm 'family' —" (and here I made sure my lip curled) "— or I'm not. And family don't have to go around thanking you for doing the cleaning and the cooking."

"Hetty can manage it."

"Oh, Hetty!" I scoffed. "Oh, of course! Hetty the Perfect! Hetty the Perfect *Pain!*"

She went bright red again.

"Go on," she said. "Be as nasty as you like. But I know which I'd choose: a child who knows how to behave, or one who doesn't."

I scowled.

"I know how to behave."

"Do you?" She raised her eyebrows. "You insist you're not 'family'" (and here she imitated my scornful voice) "but you certainly have no idea how to be-

have as a guest. You sit and take. You never stir yourself to offer to help with anything. And in all the time
that you've been coming, you've never so much as offered me a petunia picked out of a public park!"

Now it was my turn to be stung.

"I gave you a present for your birthday. And for
Christmas."

She laughed.

"Oh, yes! Soap! And then more soap! Leftovers from
your mother's gift drawer, I suppose."

I *hate* it when she mentions Mum.

"Don't do that, please!"

"Do *what?*"

She seemed genuinely astonished.

"Make snide remarks about my mother."

"Snide remarks?" She stared. "You have the nerve
to call that a snide remark? You, who've just called
my daughter a Perfect Pain! Now who's trying to have
it both ways?"

I can't *stand* it when people sneer at me. I just go
mad.

"She *is* a pain!" I yelled. "A *total* pain! Just like her
sister! In fact, if you want to know, I can't stand either of your ratty, squabbling children!"

Lucy went deathly white. But I kept on.

"To tell the truth," I bellowed, "I can't stand *anything* about this house. I don't like the people in it —
except my dad. And even he's too busy making sure
he doesn't show me any special favors to spend much
time with me!"

I couldn't help it. I burst into tears of rage.

"There's nothing to *do* here," I sobbed at her angrily. "There isn't even any point in going out because I don't have any friends around here. So I'm just stuck upstairs in this boring little bedroom, twiddling my thumbs, because all of my own stuff is back at the other house."

"But you could —"

"I can't!" I screamed at her. "You think I can, but I *can't!* Mum doesn't like me bringing my things around here. She won't admit it. But whenever she notices that something is missing, she just keeps on and on at me about it until I bring it back!"

"I didn't know —"

"*Nobody* knows!" I yelled at her. "Nobody ever *asks!* How would *you* like it? How would you like *any* of it?" I wiped my tears away angrily with my sleeve. "Being packed up every other week, and forced to sit and be polite to someone else's boring family!"

I clenched my fists and stamped.

"Not even close family! Half the time, when I'm here, I have to sit and listen to Sophie and Hetty's doddery old relations droning on and on!"

That got her.

"Now, listen! I've told you this before. Sunday is the only day when Nana and Grandpa can —"

"I don't *care!*" I howled at her. "Why *should* I care? They're not *mine*. They sit in their armchairs trying to think of more boring things to say to me, to try and cover up the fact that they've just sneaked Sophie and Hetty some money, and not given anything to me!"

Lucy went scarlet. She hadn't realized that I'd noticed that.

"You *see?*" I crowed. "You're going on at me to act like family and not give you boring old soap for Christmas. Why aren't you going on at them? I see the presents they give Sophie and Hetty. I see the poky things they give to me. But I don't blame them. In fact, I think they're *right*. We're *not* a normal family. It's only you who keeps on trying to pretend we are. It's *you* who keeps trying to have it all both ways!"

And then, to my amazement, Lucy lost her temper back.

"I'm not the only one who wants it both ways!" she shouted, sizzling with rage. "When it comes to that, I can assure you that your family walks off with the bronze, the silver and the gold!"

She jabbed at the comforter with her finger.

"You take your mother! She expects me to do everything for you while you're in this house. Everything! But do I get any support from her? I do not! And if there's anything that annoys her, who gets the blame? Your father? No. *Me,* of course. I'm in the perfect trap. I cannot do a single thing right, down to something as simple as taking you to the cinema. If I buy your ticket, I'm trying to bribe you or lure you away from her. And if I don't, I'm unspeakably mean and I'm favoring my own children. Whatever I do, I simply cannot win!"

Now she was jabbing with another finger.

"Then there's your dad. He wants it both ways too! So long as I pretend that everything's fine, then your dad's perfectly amiable. He's all smiles. But if I say anything, it's very different. If I say a single *word* about your lack of manners in this house, or your mother's continual criticism, or the fact that he hasn't got the guts to speak to either of you about the things that make life difficult for Sophie and Hetty and me, then all of a sudden it's as if *I'm* the problem, not you three! He puts this look on his face as if to say: 'If Lucy didn't get so worked up about all these little matters, everything would be fine.'"

And now she was pointing at me.

"And as for you! I thought you were supposed to be an intelligent girl! But you still manage to walk around this house as if you sincerely and honestly believed that, without me and Sophie and Hetty, everything in your life would be hunky-dory!"

She threw up her hands.

"Go on, then. Carry on. I'm used to it. Go on, all three of you, treating me as if I'm the only problem in your lives. Keep on telling yourselves that, if it weren't for the Wicked Stepmother, everything would be fine. Go on living in your dreamworld!"

I don't know what it was about her calling it a dreamworld that so annoyed me. But I was furious.

"*You're* the one in the dreamworld!" I shouted. "Playing Happy Families, and expecting everyone around you to play it, too! Well, I *won't* play. Why *should* I? You know I'm only here because I don't want to hurt my dad's feelings by saying I don't want to come here any longer."

Lucy's face crumpled.

"Oh, Pixie! How I wish —"

"Stop it!" I yelled. "Just stop it! You can't make things right by *wishing* them. You know that! That's just as silly and hopeless as me wanting you to get run over by accident, so Mum and Dad can get back together, and buy our old house back again! It isn't going to happen, and you ought to know it!"

All the blood in her face had drained away. And when she spoke, her voice was just a tiny croak.

"I *have* to keep trying," she told me. "Can't you *see*? This is my *home*. This is my *family*. If everyone's unhappy, there's no point. Everything's spoiled."

And she burst into tears.

"Everything's spoiled anyway," I told her.

And I started crying, too.

She put her arms out, and I went to her. I couldn't help it. We sat together on the bed, both of us crying our eyes out. She stroked my hair. And then something curious happened. There was a tap on the door, and Dad was there, cautiously poking his head around with an "Are you two scrappers ready for a cup of tea now?" look.

But Lucy just said to him coldly:

"Please go away."

Maybe she thought that he was interrupting. But I don't think so. I think she was just fed up with him forever staying out of things, and not facing up to what was bothering everyone, and only creeping in when he thought the trouble was over, and it was safe.

And I felt the same. Dad could have done so much more to make things easier for all of us. He could have made an effort to find out what was difficult for me, and help me explain to Mum and to Lucy. He could have stuck up for me when I was right (and maybe even for Lucy when I was wrong). But instead he just got on with his own selfish, quiet life, pretending he didn't notice things, or leaving them for Lucy, and never trying to sort out any of the horrible, horrible mess he'd made by changing all our lives forever.

Lucy was trying hard enough. Why couldn't he?

So I stuck up for her.

"Yes, go away."

He didn't need telling twice. He disappeared. And Lucy squeezed me tight.

"Better?"

I sniffed.

"A bit," I said. And then I added, because it was true: "I wouldn't want to be a stepmother."

She squeezed me again.

"And I wouldn't want to be in your shoes." She shrugged. "But then again, I wouldn't choose to be all sorts of people. And most of them end up managing somehow."

I blew my nose.

"Lucy, what I said about not wanting to come except for not hurting Dad's feelings, that's not exactly true.

Sometimes, when Mum's going on at me, I wish I could come and live here all the time. So I can't hate it that much." I blew my nose again. "It's just that, whenever Hetty teases me about my name, or something, I want to go straight home again and never come back."

"Teases you? About your name?"

"Calls me 'Priscilla.'"

Lucy looked baffled.

"How is that teasing?"

My tears welled up again.

"*Priscilla!*" I wailed.

She took me by the elbows and shook me gently.

"Priscilla's a *beautiful* name," she told me. "And so is Cilla. I think your parents did a *lovely* job of choosing what to call you."

And somehow, because we'd finished up with Lucy saying something nice about both Mum and Dad, it felt as if the quarrel was over, with no bad feelings simmering away. I dried my tears and blew my nose again. Then I helped Lucy drag Hetty's bed back over the landing into Sophie's room.

"I don't *mind*," I kept saying. "She can stay with me if she wants."

Lucy was firm.

"No," she said. "You obviously *do* mind. So let's go back to how we were before, and if you ever change your mind, and want Hetty back, all you have to do is tell me."

"All right," I said, pulling the bedcovers straight again. "All right."

So now we're back exactly how we were before. Except that everything's different. I'm not pretending anymore. Everyone knows how I feel, and I know how they feel. We're not just playing Happy Families. (I know that Lucy still hopes we'll turn into one, but now at least she's letting us take our time.)

I'm still not crazy about my stepsisters. Hetty's a real pain, and Sophie still gets on my nerves. But we're managing better. For one thing, Hetty no longer yodels "Priscilla!" up the stairs at me. Lucy's stopped that. And, in return, I come down a lot more often than I did, and try to be more sociable. And if I'm cunning, and bring down my books, I get some help with my homework. When I said that Hetty could explain things, I really meant it. I've understood a lot of math for the first time since Hetty went over it with me. Miss O'Dell even told me last week that if I keep on like this, I might move up a set next term.

And, in return, I frighten Hetty out of her wits. Each bedtime she creeps in and perches on the end of my comforter.

"Tell me some more about the ghost of Henrietta Forbes."

"I've told you everything," I insist. "I've told you about the time her ghost appeared at the bus stop, dripping great clots of blood, with her half-severed arm still clutching her bus pass."

She nods.

"And I've told you about the time the puppies in the pet shop were found in the morning, stark staring mad, whining frantically and clawing at the bars whenever they were shown her photograph?"

She nods again. "Yes, that was a good one. I could fetch Sophie and you could tell that one again."

I shook my head. I hate telling the same story twice.

"Well, what about the time her bloodied corpse was found in the graveyard in the moonlight, sobbing and shrieking and scrabbling at her husband's grave. Have I told you that one?"

"No. Not yet."

"I'm sure I have."

"No, really, Pix. You haven't."

She bunches up the feet end of my comforter, and wraps it around her, ready for a fright. "Go on. Tell me the story."

It's better than listening to her read and sniff. So off I go.

"*One horrid dark and stormy night . . .*"

After, she sometimes goes back to her room. But only if Sophie's there. If Sophie's gone to sleep over at somebody's party, or at Nana and Grandpa's, then Hets has to stay with me. We drag the mattress off her bed, and drag it down the hall.

Dad hears us giggling, and comes out to watch.

"I simply don't understand why you two have to go through this performance time and again," he grumbles. "You're *ruining* that mattress. Why can't you just leave it on Pixie's floor?"

We just ignore him. We know better than that. I don't think either of us wants to push our luck. She's still a little wary of me, and I still get on with her that bit better when all the lights are out, and I don't have to watch her cocking her head to one side and fiddling with her hair, or rolling the cat like a sausage across the comforter.

But, just to tease him, one of us might mutter:

"Well, Lucy thinks . . ."

That always sends him off pretty smartly.

"Well done!" said Ralph. "I believed every single word of that."

Pixie shrugged modestly.

"Now tell us about the ghost of Henrietta Forbes."

Needing no further prompting, as usual, Pixie began.

"*One night, during a fierce storm —*"

Out of the darkness came the firm interruption:

"Not now, Pixie."

Everyone turned to peer at the lump of shadow that was Colin.

"Why not? Will it make you nervous?"

"We have to hear Rob's story now," Colin explained.

"I don't mind skipping mine," Rob said hopefully.

"Maybe you don't," said Colin. "But I really want to hear it."

"I could save it for tomorrow."

But everyone knew that, by tomorrow, each of them would have gone their separate ways with their own friends. This was the night for stories. And if Rob hadn't told them his before they finally gave in to sleep, they'd probably never hear it.

"Colin is right," said Ralph. "The ghost of Henrietta Forbes will have to wait. It's Rob's turn."

"Off you go, Rob."

"I can't. I don't know what to say. I don't know how to start."

"Easy!" said Pixie. "Start with '*My mum and dad* . . .' and see what comes out."

"If you say so," said Rob doubtfully.

And he began.

Benjy's the Problem

My mum and dad split up when I was only six, so I don't remember much. I can remember my dad kicking a hole in the kitchen door when they were arguing once. My mother was crying, and I was fiddling with the nutcrackers, so maybe it was Christmas. I don't know.

Dad came back a lot, and Mum would send Callie and me out in the garden, while they stayed in the kitchen, arguing and arguing. Callie kept going back inside to try to make them stop. But I just stayed out there, kicking the ball to myself, over and over. And, after a bit, Dad stopped coming around, and we had to start visiting him at his new place instead. I didn't mind, but Callie hated it. She said that it was cold and nasty and horrible, and the sheets felt funny. She tells me things I never realized, but, once she's come out with them, I know they're true, and I can't understand why I didn't work them out for myself in the first place. They always stick, though. I can never fade them out.

I can remember exactly which house we were walking past when she said, "Our dad went out to work for years and years to pay for a nice house and all the furniture, and now The Beard's moved in and taken everything, and it's not fair."

That's what she calls him. The Beard. I don't think he's too bad, but Callie really hates him. She says he picks on her all the time. And it is true that, when Joe first came, Mum only let him yell at us if we were doing something really stupid, like pushing wet fingers in a plug, or chasing balls into the road. She never let him interfere with family stuff, or anything to do with school. But since Benjy was born, Joe seems to have taken over. Now he goes around telling Callie and me what to do as if the fact that he is Benjy's dad makes it all right for him to lord it over us as well.

I don't mind terribly, but Callie *hates* it. Sometimes she stands behind a door and does this imitation of him under her breath.

"Brush your hair, please, Callie. It looks like a rat's nest." "Have you done your homework, Callie?" "Did you remember to lock your bike?" "Is this your mess on the floor? Would you clear it all up, please?"

She sounds just like him. Sometimes she even holds one of her furry slippers up against her chin, to be the beard.

"Callie, have you dusted the stars yet? And polished the moon? And is it your turn to wipe the grease off the sunbeams?"

Once, I fell down the stairs backward, laughing, and had to be taken to the hospital to have an x-ray of my head. But Callie won't admit it's funny. One night, when he'd been getting at her for leaving wet towels on the bathroom floor, she told me she'd put rat poison in his food if she thought she could get away with it.

And if it weren't for Benjy.

Benjy's the problem, you see. He's only three. And he's the sweetest child in the whole world. Even Callie admits that. I never thought anything about babies till Benjy was born. I thought they were just boring. But when Joe took us to visit Mum in the hospital, he scooped this tiny knitted bundle out of its little swinging plastic tub, and put it in my arms. And suddenly it sneezed — the neatest little sneeze you ever heard — and its eyes popped open in surprise, and it stared up at Joe peering over my shoulder. Joe said that Benjy was far too young to be staring at him properly. But Mum and I knew better. And Benjy's proved us right. He's been following Joe around ever since like a little baby duckling. Sometimes the twins next door borrow him for their games.

"Shove Benjy in the closet. Then, when he bangs, pretend he's the monster."

"No. Let's play prisoners. Put him in his crib."

"If we put this red hat on him, he could be Santa."

"No. Let him be a frog. Kiss him and see if he turns into a prince!"

But as soon as Benjy hears Joe coming through the gate, he struggles till they let him go, and rushes down the stairs into Joe's arms. Mum shakes her head and says, "He's definitely his dada's son." And Callie makes that little face that Joe can't stand, and whispers to me:

"Nice that he has the chance! At least he and his dada get to live in the same house!"

But I don't really mind. I think it's nice to see Joe turning Benjy upside down, and pretending to use him to vacuum the carpets. The week that Joe announced his mother was ill, and went away, Benjy was awful.

"Want Dada!"

"Dada coming home soon?"

"Make Joe come back now, Wob!"

It nearly drove me mad. By Thursday, I was halfway up the wall. When Callie heard the gate click, and said, staring out of the window, "Surprise, surprise! Here's The Beard back again," I almost felt like cheering. Benjy went tumbling down the stairs in his excitement. And Callie took great pleasure in tormenting Joe all through the evening.

"How was your mother, Joe?"

"Which hospital was she in?"

"Who else was visiting?"

"What's wrong with her, exactly?"

From all his fudging and squirming, I realized that Callie had been right all week. Joe's mother wasn't ill at all. He'd obviously had a fight with Mum, and just stormed out.

"How did you *know?*"

"I *told* you," said Callie. "Nobody ever rushes off to visit someone in the hospital without a phone call. And there was no phone call that night. Just lots of hissy whispering in their room. And Mum had red eyes in the morning. And even *you* noticed how much more polite she was to Dad on Saturday. In fact, I think . . ."

Her voice trailed off. I knew what she was thinking, and gave her a good long look, to tell her so.

She went bright red.

"It's not impossible," she said. "People *do* get back together. You never know. It might happen."

But Benjy's the problem. I'm not sure how Dad would take to looking after him, if he came back. And anyway, Joe might not want to leave his only child with someone else, especially not Dad. They might start squabbling about it, and Callie and I know only too well how horrible that can be. I couldn't bear to think of poor little Benjy sitting at the table fiddling with the nutcrackers, while everyone else is arguing around him.

But Callie still thought that it was worth a try.

"Look, you skip the weekend with Dad, and drag Mum off to the mall to get your new soccer shoes. Phone me as soon as you know what time you'll be there, and I'll think of some excuse to drag Dad out shopping. Then, when we've all bumped into one another, I'll fake a coughing fit, and make them take us in that café for a drink."

She's smart, my sister. Everything went like clockwork. We sat around one of the marble-topped tables in Ginna's Ice Cream Parlor, and Callie tried to start things off.

"Well, this *is* nice."

I backed her up.

"Like being a real family again."

"You're *in* a real family," Mum reminded me sharply.

"Don't snap at the boy, Hope," Dad said irritably. "You know exactly what he means."

And off they went, grinding away at one another as usual, with Dad wanting to know why Mum had let me skip my weekend at his house if I wasn't playing in a match, and Mum saying she was surprised that either of us ever bothered to go at all, given his grumpy moods. In the end, Callie and I slipped off our seats, and went to stand in front of the display of ice-cream cakes.

"Well," Callie said sarcastically. "This *is* going well, isn't it?"

"They're hopeless when they meet."

She turned to stare at me.

"That's it! They're hopeless when they meet. So we'll try something else!"

And so we did. The "something else" turned out to be a load of barefaced lies.

"Mum says to thank you for returning my sweater."

"Dad says it was really nice of you to send him that list of my soccer games."

"Mum says you cook much better pizzas than Joe does."

"Dad was pretty impressed by the nifty way you beat his next-door neighbor to that parking place."

We got really good at it as the weeks passed. I even began to think of myself as an ace troubleshooter, keeping the peace between two hot-blooded scrappers. And, after a while, something strange happened. Without even noticing, they started to do the job for themselves.

"Ask your dad if he'd like to have you for a couple of extra days over half-term."

"Tell your mum if she needs some new tires on that car of hers, I know a man who gets them very cheaply."

"Don't forget to take that spare fruitcake around to Daddy's house."

"Why don't you give Mummy these plant cuttings Aunt Sue left me? I know I'll never manage to make them grow."

Callie was getting pretty confident now.

"We're doing well," she told me. "We're almost there."

But I wasn't nearly so sure. I reckoned there was still a big difference between the two of them trying to get along like reasonable people, sending each other unwanted fruitcake and plant cuttings and things, and their wanting to get back together in the same house. But I didn't want to spoil things for Callie, whose eyes lit up at every little spat between Mum and Joe.

"The Beard's in trouble again," she'd tell me, grinning. "He's planned some overtime for the evening she wanted to go out."

Or:

"Mum's ripping mad. He left the groceries lying on the table, and now that ice cream's melted in the carton."

She'd come in my room in the morning, and tell me hopefully:

"I think they had another argument last night."

I tried to warn her.

"Lots of people argue. It probably doesn't mean what you think."

"It did with Dad. And Joe has stormed out once already."

"And he came back."

But Callie had got it all worked out in her head.

"You wait and see. One day, Mum and The Beard will have a giant fight, and he'll leave, just like before. But this time, instead of moping, she'll get in touch with Dad."

Her eyes fell on the chubby little fists fighting their way out of the sleeves of a desperately flapping soccer shirt, eight sizes too big.

"Benjy's the problem, of course . . ."

Both of us watched him silently for a moment. Then Callie said:

"Well, Benjy will simply have to learn to cope. You have. And I have. So Benjy can as well."

"But Benjy's only *three*."

"He's *nearly* four."

And it was on his birthday that the big fight came. But it wasn't between Mum and Joe, when it happened.

Well, not at the start, at least. At the beginning, it was between Callie and Joe. He caught her pushing her bike down the very narrow space between the bushes and the car.

"Callie! You know you're not supposed to do that. Go around!"

"I'm in a *hurry*."

"You can't go that way. You'll scratch the car."

"No, I won't."

"Callie! I'm warning you! Come back! Right *now!*"

Callie scraped the bike fiercely along the bushes, breaking stems.

"You can't tell me what to do! You're not my father!"

He caught her by the wrist and swung her around.

"That's my car you're about to scratch!"

"It's sitting in *our* drive. By *our* house! In *our* garden!"

"Listen," he hissed in her ear. "I've just about had enough of you!"

Tears spurted out of Callie's eyes.

"And we've all had enough of *you!* You're a big, meddling *pig,* and you've nothing to do with us. You're bossy and horrible, and even Mum's sick of you!"

I think he might have slapped her then. But just at that moment Mum threw open the window.

"Joe! Let go of Callie at once, please!"

Joe stared up at her. He was open-mouthed.

"Are you taking *her* side?"

"I'm not taking any side at all," called Mum. "But *she* wants you to let go of her, and *I* want you to let go of her."

"Because she's not my daughter? Is that it?" He dropped Callie's wrist as if it had scorched him. "Well, let me tell you something, Hope. If I'm good enough to get up half an hour earlier than I need to every morning to drive her to school, and good enough to work overtime to pay for repairs to the roof over her head, and good enough to trail around the supermarket for her favorite foods, then I'm good enough to stop her carelessly scratching my car!"

Mum slammed the window shut, and that was it. The fight was on. They tried a dozen times to sort it out over the next few days. But every discussion ended with flaring tempers and banging doors, or with silence and cold looks. It seemed they couldn't come to terms at all. Joe was insisting he had every right to make Callie do what he told her. And Mum was arguing that it wouldn't help. "Believe me," I heard her say over and over. "It's better if you leave all that to me. Callie's so proud, and if you push it, all that will happen is she'll start to hate you."

Start! I could have told them both something. But I kept quiet. And slowly, slowly, the days went by. It was quite obvious that things were getting worse and worse. On Wednesday Callie was twenty minutes late for school because Joe suddenly decided he wasn't going to drive her anymore. ("I only give lifts to people who are civil to me," he announced. "And Callie barely speaks.") On Thursday, he came back without the only cereal Callie likes. ("I only shop for people who say thank you as if they mean it.") And when the snow began on Friday evening, he made it clear that even though Mum's car was in the garage being fixed, he wasn't driving us to Hawksmoor Hill with our toboggans. ("The slope in the yard's good enough for Benjy. And after all, as Callie says, you've all had enough of me.")

"Pig!" Callie muttered, gazing out at the glorious white flurries. A tear rolled down her cheek, and I knew she was remembering the time Dad hurried us out of the house into the car, and we were first on the hill. First to make tracks over the huge, perfect, winking blanket of snow. First to hurtle down the steep slopes without having to steer around people dragging their sleds up again. First in the whole white world, or so it seemed.

With her finger, Callie tracked another snow tear down the window pane.

"I wish —"

But she couldn't say it. And I pretended she'd meant something else.

"Maybe Joe will feel differently tomorrow."

She shrugged. She couldn't care.

"Maybe he will."

He didn't, though. Joe is as stubborn as Callie, in his own way. All morning he made a great show of keeping busy, clearing out the shed. Benjy trailed after him, of course, to and fro under the kitchen window, as Joe carried one armful of junk after another along to the trash cans.

Mum opened the door a crack against the icy wind. "Come inside, Benjy."

He shook his head so fiercely, his knitted hat fell on the snowy path.

Mum tried again.

"Benjy! You're freezing out there. Come in with us."

Callie and I watched from the window as Benjy turned his back and stamped off.

"Joe! Send Benjy in, please! He's blue with cold."

Joe just pretended not to hear, and disappeared into the shed.

Pulling her boots on, Mum went after them. Callie opened the window, so she could listen better. Blasts of wind swept in, lifting her hair, and gobs of sleet blew in her face, but she didn't notice. She was determined to hear every word.

"Joe!" Mum rattled the latch of the shed door. "Joe! Can you please persuade Benjy to come back inside."

Joe poked his head out.

"I think it's obvious he wants to stay with me."

Mum stood her ground.

"It's very cold. I'd like him back inside, please."

"Why? Aren't two children out of three enough for you?"

Mum told him, icy as the wind that swirled sleet in her face:

"That's a ridiculous thing to say. It's not a matter of Benjy's taking sides."

Joe lifted another box of broken plastic plant pots.

"I don't see why not. *You* obviously have. So he can, too."

"What's that supposed to mean?"

Joe didn't answer, so Mum turned to Benjy, who was standing forlornly in the snow, sucking a sodden mitten.

"Come with me, Benjy."

Benjy looked anxiously at Joe, who simply handed him a little pile of plastic flowerpots to carry to the trash cans.

Beside me, Callie hissed:

"The Beard's a pig! An interfering pig! I hope he stays out all day and freezes to death!"

But Benjy was the problem. For just a moment it looked as if Mum might lose her patience and reach down to snatch him up. But she thought better of it. All of us know it's almost impossible to keep Benjy from Joe's side when he's at home. And anyway, I don't think she could face the idea of Joe watching her carrying him, screaming and thrashing, back to the kitchen.

So in the end she simply said to Joe, with as much dignity as she could muster:

"I hope you'll come to your senses in a few minutes, and bring him in."

He didn't, though. The two of them had carried at least three more loads to the trash cans before Mum cracked.

"Rob," she said to me. "Please try and get him to come in for me."

I had a go. I took the tiny pair of dry gloves Mum handed me, and went outside. The freezing wind gusted straight down the neck of my jacket. It was so cold, I played my best card first.

"Benjy, if you come in, I'll throw balls for you to head-butt."

Benjy just shook his head. I turned to Joe.

"Mum's worried about him. She wants him back inside."

Joe took the dry gloves from me.

"He's wrapped up perfectly warmly. It's only snow."

He peeled off Benjy's wet mittens, then pried open the clenched little fists to pull on the gloves. Benjy's fingers were stiff with cold, and Joe's weren't much better.

"Why are you *doing* this?" I asked. "Why choose today to clear out the shed? Benjy would follow you, if only you'd come in."

"Come in to *what*, though?" Joe asked sarcastically, before stamping off.

And I couldn't answer, because I knew exactly what he meant. Come in to a house that was colder to him, in its own way, than working in a January garden. Come in to wintry little looks, and icy silences and frosty glares.

But then I thought of something, and called after him.

"You could at least do it for Benjy's sake!"

Joe swung around. His eyes flashed to match the droplets of snow glistening in his beard.

"Don't tell *me* what to do for Benjy's sake!"
he snapped. "I'm still *here,* aren't I? Isn't *that* enough?"

I stared. It honestly hadn't ever occurred to me that,
if it weren't for Benjy, Joe might not still be in our
house. I realized for the first time that when Joe took
off that week, he hadn't intended to come back again.
Why hadn't Callie guessed that? It was the sort of thing
she always used to work out first. Perhaps she'd been
so busy wishing him gone, she hadn't noticed that, if
it weren't for Benjy, he'd have been just as glad to stay
away.

So Benjy was the problem for Joe, as well.

I think it must have worried Joe to see me staring
at him for so long, not saying anything. In the end, he
broke the silence himself.

"All right," he said. "Take Benjy in with you."

Benjy put on his stubborn look.

"Come along," I said, holding out my hand.

Benjy hid both hands behind his back. I could tell
we were in for a long haul. And so could Joe.

"What do you reckon?" he muttered to me over
Benjy's head.

"Strawberry rocket," I mouthed. (I'd tried my best
shot already, don't forget. And Benjy's passion for
Popsicles lasts all year round.)

"Okay," Joe told Benjy. "I'm sending Rob in to fetch
you a Popsicle. And when it's finished, you go back
inside. Is that a deal?"

Benjy nodded. Every toddler has his price. And then
he trailed me to the kitchen door, and stood there grin-

ning at Mum while I fetched a strawberry rocket out of the freezer.

"Right," I said, anchoring its thin stick more firmly through a hole in his glove. "As soon as that's finished, in you come."

He nodded again, and stamped off through the snow. I turned to Mum and Callie.

"Success!" I announced proudly.

Well, more fool me! The three of us stood in a line and watched for nearly an hour as Benjy outsmarted us. Not once did he stick out his tongue to take so much as a lick from that strawberry rocket. The thing stayed upright, pink and perfect on its stick. And in the icy air, colder than any freezer, it didn't even begin to melt.

"I'm going out to fetch him now," Mum kept insisting. But, though she put her boots on several times, it was quite clear she couldn't face another argument with Joe.

"He's totally *mad*," said Callie, wiping yet another viewing hole in the misted pane. "Why won't he come back in where it's warm?"

"Because he's his dada's son."

I must have heard Mum say it a thousand times. But always, before, it sounded patient and amused. This time it sounded different. It sounded trapped.

"I didn't mean Benjy," said Callie. "I meant Joe. Why won't *he* come inside?"

I honestly can't explain quite what it was that made me tell her. I'd like to kid myself it was because I'd suddenly realized Mum had had enough of being the umpire between Callie and Joe. (And how could she stop? If she gave up believing that one day the two of them might learn to live together under one roof, she'd have to ask Joe to leave. Then, either she'd lose Benjy, or Benjy would lose his precious dada.) But maybe I was as fed up as Joe with the grim atmosphere inside our house. The whole business seemed to me suddenly to have gone on far too long — like one of those soccer matches that turn to stalemate almost as soon as they begin, and drag on forever. No loose balls. No flying passes. No brilliant breakaways.

Coach always tells us: "Force it *open,* boys!"

"I'll tell you why he won't come back inside," I said. "Because he's as fed up as we are. He feels unwelcome in this house. In fact, he'd really like to leave, but Benjy's the problem."

Mum sank on the edge of a chair as if I'd punched the stuffing out of her.

"Rob! That is a *terrible* thing to say!"

You can trust Callie to come up in support when it's a chance to have a dig at Joe.

"You know you've been arguing recently," she told Mum.

"Everyone has arguments," Mum defended herself and Joe. "Children Benjy's age are tiring. Very tiring. Most of our arguments are about silly things like ice cream left to melt, and baby-sitting mix-ups. If Joe and I could only have a little break occasionally, there'd be far fewer of these little spats."

"They're not all little spats," I persisted. "Joe did walk out on us for a whole week."

Mum flushed.

"That was quite different. That was —"

Glancing at Callie, she broke off. But Callie met her eye.

"I know what you were going to say. That was about *me.*"

Mum nodded. "It isn't easy," she said. "You get upset with him. He gets upset with you. And I'm stuck in the middle." She shook her head. "Never mind. It's just a matter of time, I'm sure."

Coach says: "Keep up that pressure. Push them *hard.*"

"How can it just be a matter of time?" I argued. "Joe moved in almost as soon as Dad moved out. And you've been getting on with Dad a hundred times better than Callie's been getting on with Joe."

Mum stared at me.

"What has got *into* you today? Why are you coming out with all this?"

"Because I'm fed up with it all," I told her. "I want to start over again. New season. Fresh game."

I gave Callie a really meaningful look.

"And maybe even fresh *teams.*"

Callie stared back as if, at *last,* she'd understood what I was prodding her to try and say.

"Yes," Mum agreed. "A good idea. Let's all try again. New season. Fresh game."

I noticed she'd left out "fresh teams." And so did Callie.

"No," she said firmly to Mum. "Don't go on pretending. There's no point. I can't get on with Joe. I've tried and tried. But I can't stand him."

She saw the look on Mum's face, and her voice rose to a wail.

"Don't *look* at me like that! You know it's true. I just can't bear him. I can't bear his face, or his voice, or his beard, or anything about him. I can't stand him when he's trying to be nice, and I can't stand him when he's cross with me. I especially can't stand him telling me what to do."

The tears were pouring down her face.

"Don't tell me I'll get used to it! It isn't going to work. I know it. Rob knows it. Even Joe knows it. And, if you're honest with yourself, you know it too. I'm never going to get used to Joe. Never, ever, *ever*. He's *never* going to feel like family to me. He's like a stranger in the house."

She dropped her voice to a whisper.

"And when he's here, it doesn't even feel like home to me anymore."

I watched the second hand swing around the clock. *Don't lose it now, Callie,* I was willing her. *Go on for goal.*

Mum stretched out her arms, and Callie threw herself on her knees on the floor, and buried her head in Mum's lap. Gently, Mum patted her hair, to comfort her. Frankly, I thought it could only be the whistle now. Time up. Game over. Lost it by a hair.

But I was wrong. Callie's next words came out so muffled that neither of us could hear them properly. But they came out.

Mum stopped the patting and looked up at me.

"What did she say?"

Sometimes you have to take a risk to finish the game. I took a deep breath.

"I think she probably said she wants to go and live with Dad."

Mum looked as if I'd slapped her.

"But Callie doesn't even like your father's place! She says it's cold and gloomy, and not like a real home at all."

Callie just buried her head deeper in Mum's lap. So, once again, it was up to me.

"I think she'd still rather be there, even without us, than here with Joe."

Mum stared at the wall. Again, I watched the second hand on the clock sweep around and around. All I could hear was Callie's muffled sobbing.

And finally, finally, Mum found the courage to lift Callie's tear-streaked, stricken face.

"Do you really dislike him *that* much? Do you *really?*"

And finally, finally, Callie found the courage to nod.

So there we are. My sister's moving to Dad's house at the end of next week. She'll have to change schools, but not even that's going to stop her. Mum's spent the last few weeks reading poor Dad the riot act about checking Callie's homework properly, and not letting her out with her friends on any school nights. And his whole house has been done over, too. Mum's been over there a dozen times, changing Dad's curtains for nicer ones "because they're warmer and Callie easily catches cold," and putting pictures and photos and plants all over "because they're Callie's favorites," and even dragging Dad on shopping trips to the mall.

"Because Callie's very interested in new bath mats and table lamps," Dad said sarcastically.

But you could tell he didn't really mind. I think that, in a way, he was relieved that Mum was helping him make the place look more like a home.

"Right," Mum said last night, as she dumped Callie's new sheets and blankets on the bed. "I'm finished now. I think you're properly organized."

Dad followed her back into his new cosy sitting room.

"You'll need a holiday after all this work."

"Fat chance," scoffed Mum. "You could look after Rob, of course. But Benjy's the problem."

I looked at Callie. Callie looked at me. She knew she owed me one. Like Dad, she knows it hasn't been easy for Mum, over the last few weeks, telling the school, explaining to her friends, comforting me.

"We could look after Benjy here," she said.

Instantly, I charged up behind her in support.

"Yes. Why not? He'd love it here with us. He'd have a ball."

I realize Dad could hardly have made a fuss. Not after all Mum's work. But even I thought he showed far more enthusiasm than he need. His eyes lit up. "Yes! Why don't you and Joe go off together somewhere very soon? I'm sure the two of you could do with a nice break."

So much for Callie's dreams of mended love! But still, she didn't seem to mind. She watched him pat Mum's hand, and say,

"Yes, you leave Benjy here with us. He'll be no problem."

And she just grinned.

"That's right," she said. "Benjy's no problem. None at all."

See? Coach is right. New season. Fresh teams. Brand-new game.

Surprised, both by himself and by the tale he'd told, Rob raised both arms in a victory salute.

"I did it! Pixie told me to start with 'My mum and dad . . .' and out it all came. My story!"

Ralph tactfully let the moment of triumph pass before pointing out:

"It was your sister's story, really."

"Same thing."

"No. That's not true." Ralph reached for the album lying on Pixie's bed. "Your sister has more in common with Richard Harwick than with you. Both of them can't stand their stepfathers. Both of them have to leave. And you're not like that."

"So I'm like little Charlotte, am I?"

Ralph grinned.

"No. I'm just saying Callie's story isn't yours. Everyone's story is different."

There was a fresh patter of rain against the windows as Rob thought about it. Then he asked Ralph:

"Do you think Callie really ought to stay?"

"No." Ralph's surprise was evident. "Why?"

Rob shrugged.

"You know . . . Being like Richard Clayton Harwick . . . Running away . . ."

Ralph told him fiercely:

"You mustn't say that! Your sister isn't running away. She's simply trying something different to make things work. She's only doing what everyone has to do, over and over. I've done it. Pixie's done it. So has Claudia. You heard their stories." He swung his arm around. "And even Colin, when he finally runs away, is going off to find something that worked for him before. He's not just going to *disappear*."

He caught the look of unease that flitted over Colin's face.

"Are you?" he demanded.

There was no answer.

"*Are* you?" he said again.

"Ralph," Claudia said softly. "Better leave it."

Ralph waved away the warning.

"You saw his face. He isn't simply running off to find his stepdad. He plans to *disappear*."

"How else is he supposed to run away?" Rob demanded.

Ralph answered irritably:

"Don't be so dense. There must be a dozen ways to keep in touch without letting anyone find you, and drag you back. And Colin's probably thought of all of them. He's had enough time."

"Maybe that's the point." Pixie defended Colin. "Maybe he's had too much time. Maybe he thinks that now it's his mother's turn to sit at home missing someone horribly, wondering where they are, and what they're doing."

Ralph spread his hands.

"I understand how he feels. But he can't do that."

"Why can't I?" Colin asked him sullenly.

"Because, like Richard Harwick said, you'd just be piling one wrong onto another, till everything was broken from the strain."

"She should know how it feels," Colin insisted stubbornly.

Ralph's voice was very much gentler now.

"Misery isn't a baton in a relay race," he said. "You can't get rid of it just by passing it on."

"You don't know anything about it."

"I know what everybody knows," insisted Ralph. "Unhappiness works like one of those huge snowballs you see in parks. The more you roll it around and around, the more there is of it. And your tiny bit that started it stays in the middle, cold and hard, where you can't get at it anymore. And where it lasts the longest."

He snatched up the album.

"That's why I'm glad that Richard Clayton Harwick isn't here tonight. I'm glad we didn't have to sit and listen to him telling his story. I might have told him something. I might have said that he didn't try hard enough and he didn't try long enough. He just threw in his chips and made a ruin of his house and home."

Colin was unconvinced.

"And what's so wrong with that?"

Ralph spun the pages through his fingers.

"What's wrong with that? I'll tell you what's wrong with that. It means he was behaving no better than them!"

He tossed the album back on the bed.

"*Somebody* has to make the effort," he reminded them. "And, as we all know, the ones who mess everything up in the first place aren't quite so good at fixing things again after."

The longest silence fell. Pixie reached for the album and turned the pages over, one by one. Colin stared stubbornly out of the window at the gray ribbon of cloud lightening steadily to pink. Rob inspected his fingers, and Claudia watched Ralph. Outside, the stain of darkness gradually slipped away, and the faded stripes on the far wall were suddenly shot with silver.

Claudia spoke.

"It's time to put it back."

Without a word, Pixie handed her the faded binder. Rob pushed open the false section of wall, and Ralph followed Claudia into the little tower room. Gently, he spun the globe as he went by. The quiet rumble filled the room as Claudia first laid the album back on the spindly wooden desk, then, changing her mind, pulled out the drawer beneath and slipped it safely away, far at the back, well out of sight. When she drew out her fingers, she held a tiny splinter of wood.

"What's that?"

"The leg from Charlotte's little wooden cow."

"Oh. Right."

Ralph turned away and sprang the window catch. It moved as easily as if he'd done it yesterday, a hundred years ago, and all the days and nights between. Far, far beneath, the driveway wound into the dark of the shrubbery. The lawns lay shrouded in the silver mist. Somewhere, an owl hooted.

"He *could* have tried again," insisted Ralph.

She came to join him at the window.

"Perhaps he thought he was the only one."

Ralph's voice was thick with scorn.

"How could he think he was the only one? Stories from the old days are knee-deep in stepmothers and stepfathers!"

Claudia picked up the little wooden cow and stroked its nose.

"Everyone thinks that they're the only one. You ought to know that."

She held the little leg against the cow.

"He could have fixed that, too," Ralph told her irritably.

Claudia took one last deep breath of cool, damp air.

"*Daylight creeps over the sill,*" she said, remembering. "Come on. Let's do what Richard Harwick says. Let's leave it to the spiders in their webs to argue\ whether he was right or wrong."

Ralph pointed to the little cow.

"Better leave that."

But Claudia tightened her fingers around it.

"I was just thinking," she said, opening her other hand to show the broken leg. "I was just thinking maybe Richard Harwick wouldn't mind if we gave this to someone who'll need a bit of practice fixing things."

Ralph pulled the window shut, and turned the latch.

"Do you mean Colin?"

She nodded.

"Here. Give it to me."

This time she followed him, out of the room. Carefully, she pulled the door closed behind her. The shaft of bright dawn light had slid across the wall, leaving the telltale pockmark in shadow again, invisible, inviolate. Pixie had disappeared upstairs. Colin was already asleep. And Rob watched in silence as Ralph thrust the precious little wooden cow and its small leg deep into Colin's bag.

And then he grinned.

"It's not exactly a bluebird, is it?" he said to Ralph. "But it might work."

And, not expecting any answer, he drew the coverlet over his head as Claudia crept quietly from the room.